TWICE THE PROBLEMS

ATLANTIC CITY'S MOST WANTED #5

CHARITY PARKERSON

PUNK & SISSY PUBLICATIONS

COPYRIGHT

—Warning: This book is intended for readers over the age of 18. Some of my books contain allusions to past abuse and trauma.

Contents

INTRODUCTION

ONCE A NOTORIOUS GOLD digger, Salem got that gold... and his dead husband's grown stepsons. He has a problem.

After Salem's husband passed, leaving him a billionaire, he should've gotten to quietly live the unbothered life he always dreamed of having. Unfortunately, Salem was nowhere near JD's first spouse. Two of his past marriages left him an ex-stepson apiece, but JD had loved the boys like his own. That leaves Salem the responsibility of caring for them. Make no mistake, they're grown men, but the pair are also what people might describe as pretty but too dumb to live. Salem couldn't love them more.

Dodge and Quest have been best friends for years. JD was a good parent to them, even after he technically wasn't their dad anymore. Thankfully, JD didn't leave them with nothing when he passed. Their one-third of his enormous beachside mansion means they don't have to leave their home... or Salem. Every day of living with Salem brings them closer to feelings they never expected. They're not opposed to sharing. Now they just need to convince Salem to see them as more than a responsibility. That'll be the tricky part.

Twice the Problems is the fifth book in Charity Parkerson's Atlantic City's Most Wanted series. These are sexy and sometimes dark stories where the richest and most danger-ous men in Atlantic City meet their match. These are best enjoyed when read in order.

AUTHOR NOTE

THIS IS A DARK romance series, including murder, abuse, drug use, and crime lords.

CHAPTER ONE

THE SCENT OF EXPENSIVE cologne wafted over Dodge before he saw him. Salem. Wow. He was beautiful in a way Dodge hadn't encountered before three years ago when the guy married Dodge's dad. Well, stepdad. Dodge's mom had married JD when Dodge was sixteen. His stepson from a previous marriage had already lived here. Meeting Quest was a different story. Salem was the one who caught him totally by surprise. Dark

5

blond hair, slim body, and pouty lips came together to create perfection. He supposed that was what it took to catch the eye of a ninety-year-old billionaire and be married in under a month. Hell, JD had gone on vacation to the greyhound track in Pensacola to bet on the races. That was how short their dating relationship had been. Three weeks in Florida and JD had come home wearing a wedding band and smiling like a fucking idiot. The guy had smiled like that every day until his heart gave out in under six months. Since he left a majority of his wealth to Salem, Quest and he might have contested the will, except they had been here every day of that marriage. Not only had JD been happier than Dodge had ever seen him, but his mind had also been sound. JD's money ended up exactly where he wanted it to go. Thankfully, Salem was the greatest person—next to Quest—Dodge had ever met. Unfortunately, the guy made Dodge feel things, and he didn't know where to go with that.

Salem's gorgeous smile lit the room when he spotted Dodge sprawled out on the couch. "Hello, beautiful."

"Hi." God, how did Salem not hear the longing, happiness, and love in every word Dodge said?

He watched Salem cross the room. His heart beat faster with every step.

Salem bent and kissed his forehead. "What's wrong? It's not like you to be home this time of day. Did they close the gym?" Salem's laughter took the sting from the question. He hated that was all anyone thought he was: a gym bro with nothing else to offer except a nice body. That was probably true, but fuck. He wanted Salem to see him differently. Dodge knew he did, but today, his thoughts were ugly.

Dodge shrugged. "I guess I'm kind of bored with life today. Why do you smell so good? Are you going somewhere? Can I come?" Damn, he really wanted Salem to make him come. Dodge wanted to slap himself. Why was he like this with Salem?

"You think I smell good? Awww. Thank you. Shaw is coming by to take me to coffee."

Dodge nearly groaned. They had met Shaw Howe at their old roommate Tarek's wedding. The guy was a big-time lawyer. Like everyone, Shaw eyed Salem like a starving man watching his meal cook in the microwave. The impatient hunger made Dodge want to punch him in his objectively handsome face.

Dodge rolled from the couch. "Welp, there's my cue. I guess I'll see if Quest wants to do something."

Salem touched his arm, stopping him before he got away. His gaze moved over Dodge's face, looking into his soul the way only Salem did. "What's wrong, sweetie? You know you can talk to me about anything. Do you not like Shaw? I trust your judgment of people."

He was so amazing. Salem was the only person other than Quest who didn't treat him like an idiot. Dodge shook his head. He felt guilty for making Salem consider his feelings at all. "Nah. It's not that. He's just a lot smarter than me and I don't know." He shrugged.

"Don't say things like that. Don't compare yourself to anyone else. There's no one out there as beautiful as you, and that has nothing to do with looks."

Dodge dipped his head. He never knew what to say when Salem said things like that. Dodge knew he was just being kind, but it still made him feel good. "Seriously. Go enjoy your date or whatever."

Salem kissed his cheek. "It's not a date. It's coffee."

Dodge forced a smile and bit his tongue. Coffee was a date, but whatever. He walked away. He couldn't think straight when Salem stood too close. Dodge needed to find Quest. Quest understood him like no one.

Quest's bedroom light was off, and the curtains drawn. Dodge never knocked. They were closer than a closed door.

He crawled into bed with Quest. "Why are you still sleeping?"

A throaty chuckle came from beneath Quest's pillow. The sound made Dodge smile—the way it always did. "Hangover."

"Ah. I'll talk softly."

Dodge swore he heard Quest smile. "You're good. You know I find you soothing."

Quest always made Dodge feel cherished. Dodge knew he wasn't special. He was a pretty face and muscular body. Nobody wanted to hear his thoughts or asked his opinion. From the day they met, Quest had been different. Dodge couldn't imagine life without him.

"I have something I need to talk about, but I don't know where to start. My head is kind of a mess about it."

"Salem."

Dodge was taken aback. He didn't respond.

Another chuckle caressed his ears. Quest appeared from beneath the pillow and tucked it beneath his head. On his side, facing Dodge, he gave Dodge his full attention. "I know. He's..."

"Yeah," Dodge said, totally under-standing. "You too, huh?" Dodge wasn't surprised. He had seen the way Quest looked at Salem. They had similar tastes. Always had.

Quest's feet brushed his. Silence grew between them. Neither of them want-ed to be the first to admit how badly they wanted this.

Dodge was the first to break. "The usual rules?"

A bark of laughter burst from Quest. "We're talking about Salem here. I think we'll have to wing it a bit."

They shared a smile. Dodge finally felt a hint of peace. Quest had him. Everything would be okay.

Salem thought too much about Dodge. Why had he looked so sad? He wished Quest had been awake when he left. Salem knew those two always had each other's back. For nearly a decade, they had been two peas in a pod. Now they were three. Salem fought a smile at the idea. Sitting alone in a booth at a coffee shop wasn't the place to smile too much. He didn't want to look insane. Really, though. Before those two, Salem hadn't known what it was like to have anyone love him for real. But that was just who they were, two freaking amazing people.

Of course, JD had always been a fantastic judge of character. He had known who to keep and who to throw away. When Quest was seven, JD had married his mom. Ten years later, they divorced. Quest had wanted to stay with JD, the only real father he had ever known. Since he was seventeen, the decision had been his to make, and JD loved him every bit as much as he would a biological son.

Two years later, JD married Dodge's mom. Dodge was seventeen and anticipated a ton of resentment and hatred from the older stepbrother who likely didn't want him. Instead, it was like they met their person and had been inseparable ever since. Unfortunately, Dodge's mom had died in a freak riding accident shortly after marrying JD, leaving Dodge nowhere else to go. Once again, JD loved the son he had gained. He never gave the pair a reason to leave. Their content life was interrupted once again six years later when JD came home from vacation with a new husband, Salem. Thankfully, Quest and Dodge were rays of light and positivity. They had welcomed Salem with a love Salem hadn't had before them. Now, three years later, Salem would walk through fire for them, which circled all the way back to wondering what the hell was going on with Dodge.

A cup appeared in front of Salem. "Black coffee, as requested, since you're obviously a masochist." Shaw slid into the booth across from him.

It was impossible not to smile. Shaw bled charisma. Salem imagined that made him a good lawyer. "My grand–father always said real men only drink their coffee black." His south–ern accent came out hard. He tried reeling it in. "I don't give a shit about any of that, of course. It's just that's all he let me have. Now anything else tastes too sweet."

Shaw's dark green gaze moved over Salem's features—like studying for a test. "I forget you're from Mississip–

pi until that accent peeks out and re-minds me."

"Actually, I'm from Louisiana." This time, Salem purposely allowed his accent to shine.

A sigh-worthy smile appeared. "A Louisiana boy named Salem. Did you live in New Orleans?"

Salem despised talking about his past, but he understood that was how people got to know each other. "No. My mom was a witch. Of course, the only thing she had cooking in her cauldron was meth. That's how I ended up in Mississippi, living with my grandfather. He was the only relative willing to take me when CPS came calling."

"I'm sorry to hear that."

Shaw's sympathy made Salem want to growl. This was why he hated these conversations. He was no one to pity. Salem shrugged. "It doesn't matter now. I'm here, living my best life. Where I came from matters not at all." Salem knew that wasn't true. Where he came from would always follow him, but he wasn't weak. "What about you? Have you always lived in this area?"

"Not too far. I was born in Pennsylvania before going to Yale. From there, my career took me all over New England until I came to work at my dad's practice here."

Salem chuckled. "Ah. Who can resist all the wealthy criminals in this town?"

"Attorney-client privilege," Shaw said with a sexy laugh.

Salem shrugged. "Big money is never clean money."

Shaw's smile never dimmed. "Except for maybe yours. JD was an honest businessman."

Salem sipped his coffee before responding. "I'm not JD." It was a test. Shaw likely knew it. Salem was used to being treated like a gold digger, but he didn't have to spend his time with people who thought badly of him.

"I knew JD pretty well. He never chose anyone to be in his life on a whim. JD saw something in other people where no one else might. He was a hell of a judge of character. If he left everything in your hands, he had a good reason. He saw something in you."

Every word Shaw spoke was likely bullshit. He was a lawyer, after all. But it was nice being treated like more than trash that married for money and won the lotto. "Not everything. You forget his stepsons."

Shaw laughed. "I doubt JD left much to them specifically. No doubt he put you in charge of their shares. There's no way those two could handle a fortune landing on their heads."

It was true, and Shaw was right. Basically, every dime had been left to him with a stipulation: he always care for Quest and Dodge like the puppies they were. Still, Shaw's words chafed. He didn't like anyone treating his boys like they were dumb. "They're not stupid or incapable. They're just too nice to be in charge of the kind of money JD had. He knew they'd be eaten alive by ladder climbers and every other piece of shit within a thousand miles.

They have too good of hearts for this world." Salem heard the papa bear in his voice. He couldn't help it. Quest and Dodge were his. No one would insult them.

Shaw looked thoughtful. "I can't tell if your fierce defense is fatherly or something else. Either way, they're lucky to have you, and I meant no offense. I was just saying—badly, apparently—the same thing as you. They're not meant for the world you and I see."

Salem's shoulders relaxed. He felt kind of dumb. People loved to treat Dodge and Quest like idiots. It enraged Salem. A guilty smile tugged at his lips. "Sorry. Since marrying

JD, I've run into way too many people who speak badly of his boys. They were the light of his life. He would've destroyed anyone who thought about insulting them. I suppose that's something else he left to me."

Shaw's expression took on a new dimension, as if Salem watched the powerful attorney rise to the surface. "It's odd. If he hadn't been a ninety-year-old billionaire, I'd say it sounds like you loved him very much."

His hackles more than rose. They flew. "Oh, there it is. I'll admit you made it much longer than expected. Thank you for the coffee. It's been a pleasure." He moved to slide from the booth.

"Did I offend you, or are you just looking to be offended?"

The question pissed him off just enough to stay to answer. "Can't it be both? Yes, I stay on constant guard to be treated exactly as you're treating me now. But yeah, I'm also highly insulted nonetheless, because despite what everyone thinks, I loved JD. Maybe it wasn't the way a husband loves his spouse, but I did love him. He was a good man who took me in, loved me, and cares for me still to this day with his legacy. Everyone in this goddamn town can think what they want, but this is exactly why I have nothing to do with any of you. Any time any of you say shit about me, you insult him. He knew exactly what he was doing when he left everything to me, and it didn't have a damn thing to do with his dick. Just because that might be all you think with, it doesn't mean everyone is like that."

Shaw's eyebrow rose. "Someone like me doesn't get where they are by thinking with their dick. I sure as hell didn't get here by judging people. In fact, I give no fucks why JD left that money to you. I don't even give a fuck about the money. It's you I want to know, but goddamn, you have a thorny personality to get past."

Despite everything, a laugh burst from Salem. His shoulders relaxed. "You're not wrong." He took a breath. It was possible he overreacted. "It's just this goddamn community. I'm a hot topic, which is fine, but I don't care to take an active part."

Shaw nodded. "I get it. The upper crust has a way of being incredibly intolerable. I'm only on the fringes, keeping their money safe and their asses out of jail. That's a close enough view that I can say with certainty I have no desire to delve deeper than the edge. Because... yikes."

Salem laughed. Damn. He felt like an idiot twice on one coffee date. "I'll bet this entire experience has left you twice as confused about why JD wanted me."

Shaw's smile disappeared. Heat flared in his expression. "Not at all. I imagine he saw exactly what I do; a sexy, highly intelligent person with tons of fire and backbone. That would've been irresistible to him. I know it is for me."

Well, fuck. It seemed he would be staying for coffee after all. Miracles never ceased.

Chapter Two

It wasn't uncommon for the three of them to exist in silence together. Life felt comfortable. They didn't have to talk. Tonight was different, though. Quest looked Dodge's way. A small smile appeared on Dodge's lips. They knew each other too well. They were too much alike.

"We should go out. It's been a while since we cut loose."

Salem snorted at Dodge's statement. "You two cut loose damn near every night."

"I meant as a family. Come to the titty bar with us."

The look Salem gave Dodge had Quest fighting back a laugh. No one could goad Salem into shit like Dodge. There was no way Dodge wanted to go to a strip club. He hated anything that sexually exploited others. "I don't want to go to a titty bar. What if I asked you to go dancing with me at a gay club? We don't have the same idea of fun."

Dodge shrugged. "I'd go dancing with you. I don't give a shit if it's a gay club."

"Okay. How about this?" Quest said, jumping into the conversation. "Let's flip a coin. Heads, strip club. Tails, gay dancing."

Salem snorted again. Quest knew that could mean anything with Salem.

Dodge dug a coin from his pocket and flipped it in the air before anyone agreed or argued. "Gay dancing, it is." He shoved the coin back in his pocket.

Quest hid a smile. He knew damn well that coin had not come up tails. Quest stood. "Well, get your shoes."

Salem didn't immediately move. He motioned at Dodge and Quest. "You're just going to go in shorts and a tank top?"

Quest and Dodge shrugged.

With a sigh, Salem stood. "You're right. Every guy there will take one look at you and drool no matter what you're wearing. Let it be on your heads, then."

Quest headed for the door before Salem thought things through and changed his mind. "I'll drive so you two can drink. I'm still hungover from last night."

Salem scoffed. "Since when has that stopped you?"

"Many times, I'll have you know." He flashed a smirk Salem's way. "Plus, I have a feeling I'll need to stay sober to protect you."

Salem shook his head as they stepped into the garage. "Definitely. People will trample all over me to get to you."

There it was. The second comment in one conversation. How could anyone resist the constant ego stroke or the hint of jealousy? Dodge held open the door of Quest's Ram quad cab. After Salem climbed into the passenger seat, Dodge climbed into the back.

"Where am I headed, exactly?"

"The Three-Legged Cowboy is decent."

A chortle came from the backseat. "The Three-Legged Cowboy."

"Hey. You boys wanted gay. We're going gay." The smile in his voice couldn't be missed.

Quest fought not to laugh. Following Salem's directions, Quest easily found the nightclub. Neon lights lit the building like Christmas. Music poured from the club into the parking lot. People practically burst from the seams. Dodge jumped out and opened Salem's door. The pair always took care of each other. Quest wasn't even sure if they noticed how much each did for the other, like it was second nature. Quest waited for the pair. They headed for the door together. Heads turned their way. Gazes swept their bodies. Open, hungry stares followed them as they stepped inside. Quest paid the cover charge.

They barely made it three steps inside before a guy in a leather harness blocked his path. "Hey, gorgeous. Can I buy you a drink?"

Quest motioned over his shoulder at Salem. "I'm with him."

The guy's leer moved past him. "What about your other friend?"

"We're all together."

"Mmm. Goddamn. I'd buy a ticket to that show."

He was about to get one. Dodge already steered them toward the dance floor and they fully intended to open Salem's eyes and toy with his lust. The moment the music engulfed him, and they had Salem between them, it was as if everyone else vanished. Quest's hips moved to the music. He held Salem's waist. His thumbs found their way beneath his shirt, caressing the bare skin above the waistband of his pants. With his back braced against Dodge's chest, Salem's gaze never wavered from holding Quest's stare. Dodge had his forearm across Salem's sternum and his nose buried against the side of Salem's neck. Smell was one of Dodge's weaknesses. Touch was

Quest's, and Salem felt damn good beneath his hands, moving to the music.

Even in the low lighting, Quest saw the desire etching Salem's every line. Maybe he would never admit it, even to himself, but Salem wanted them. Time slipped away as their bodies moved together. Then the music slowed and the space between them ceased to exist. Dodge and Quest kept Salem pinned between them. The loud music didn't hide the way their breathing got more ragged by the second.

Quest touched his mouth to Salem's ear. "See? Straight club. Gay club. It doesn't matter where we go. It'll always just be us. Are you ready to go home?"

He felt Salem nod.

Quest grabbed Salem's hand and headed for the door. He dodged men without looking their way and played deaf all the way to the truck. Quest wasn't joking. All hours of the day. Seven days a week. It was only the three of them. Salem had never asked why Quest drank so much or why Dodge continually got high. They had spent three years in hell, trying to find their footing while simultaneously knowing exactly where they were meant to be. It was frustrating and draining. Salem had the hardest shell of anyone he had ever met.

The time had come, though. Dodge's patience was gone. Salem had to face the truth. It had always been them.

Salem couldn't breathe. He needed space. The way Quest had stared at him on that dance floor and the way Dodge's lips had kept skimming his neck. Damn. It was like ants crawled all over his skin, driving him crazy with the need to act. He just hadn't decided what that action would be quite yet, but he knew damn well it would blow his life to pieces.

The ride home was made in silence. He might have run for the safety of his bedroom, if Dodge hadn't started talking and acting as if nothing happened.

"Get your pajamas on and meet us in Quest's room. It's time to play Two Dares."

"Oh, Jesus. Should I ask?"

Quest looked his way. A too-satisfied smile stretched his lips. "Probably, but you're playing nonetheless. It's our latest release."

Fuck. Salem couldn't say no. One reason the pair of stepsons had never left each other was they worked together. They created card games that were hugely successful. Most people thought they just partied on their inheritance. Truthfully, they had made a fortune by simply brainstorming together nonstop. They created various party games, drinking games, and even a few family-friendly ones. Two Dares didn't sound like kids should be playing. Quest was right, though. No matter how badly Salem wanted to run, he wouldn't. He would support his boys through every venture. They meant too much to him for him to ever let them down. If that meant gritting his teeth through their substantial charms, that was what he would do. Tomorrow, he would find a way to distance himself. Maybe he should just fuck the sexy lawyer. That was all this was. He had gone too long without someone warming his bed. Now he desperately wanted to set his life on fire.

"All right. Give me a few."

"Don't take long. I'll come after you. You'll end up over my shoulder."

"And across my lap," Quest added to Dodge's threat. His words were almost too quiet to understand.

Salem wasn't sure if he hoped he'd heard correctly or not. Either way, he hurried to the safety of his bedroom and quickly found a pair of soft pajama pants and a T-shirt. Dodge one hundred percent would barge in and throw Salem over his shoulder if he didn't get there as fast as Dodge expected. And Quest... well, Salem didn't know about his warning.

Salem had to climb the stairs to the second floor of their three-story beach home to get to Quest's bedroom. While JD had been a spry ninety, he still needed a main-floor master. Light flooded into the darkened hallway from Quest's open bedroom door. He peeked inside. Dodge was on his side, wearing workout shorts and a tank top with armholes so wide, they showed off his chest. Quest sat on the other side of a box of cards on the bed. He was dressed the same. Salem ambled inside. Two heads turned his way. One blond and the other dark. Both had amazing eyes. Salem's stomach quivered. Tonight wasn't a good night for this. Then they smiled, equally excited to see him, and they became his puppies again. His favorite humans. Salem's shoulders relaxed.

He climbed on the bed. "So, how does this work?"

Quest passed him a bottle of wine. "First, drink."

Salem turned the bottle up and took a swig before passing it back. "That's not good. Sounds like you think I'll need fortification."

Dodge laughed.

Quest set the bottle on the bedside table. "Nah. You just look like you need to loosen up a hair to enjoy yourself."

Dodge spoke up. "For the game, you just draw a card and read aloud the two options. You have to do one. After you do, you put the card at the back of the deck. If you choose to do neither, you keep the card. The first person to keep three cards is out. So on and so forth until one player is left standing."

That didn't sound terrible. "Okay. Who goes first?"

"Whoever is oldest goes first. Then clockwise."

As Quest answered, he drew a card. Technically, he was only three days older than Salem, but technical was what mattered in games. He read the card he held. "Take off your shirt and bra, if applicable, or ask the person on your left to describe their underwear." Quest peeled off his shirt and tossed it on the floor.

Salem nearly groaned. Maybe this would be hell.

Dodge snickered. "It said ask. I didn't have to tell you to meet the perimeter."

Quest shrugged and put the card back. His expression stayed serious. "I already know you're not wearing underwear. You never do. No need to go there."

Dodge shrugged and drew a card. "Twerk for fifteen seconds or lick the bottom of the person on your left's foot."

Salem's spine straightened. He could watch some twerking.

Dodge sat up, grabbed Salem's foot and licked it, making Salem squeal. He roared with laughter at Salem's reaction.

Indignant and turned on, Salem snatched up the next card, praying it was a way he could take revenge. "Confess your deepest desire or your greatest fear." Well, fuck.

Dodge turned serious. "You don't have to do that one. We'll give you a pass."

Salem shook his head and put the card back. "That's an easy one. My biggest fear is losing you two."

For a moment, silence fell over them. Salem didn't look at anyone. Finally, he broke. "I believe it's your turn again, Quest."

Quest drew a card. "French kiss the person to your left or call your mom and describe losing your virginity in painful detail. Uh, yeah. Fuck that cunt." He looked Dodge's way.

Dodge smiled like an idiot.

Quest shrugged and the next thing Salem knew, he watched the hottest fucking kiss he had ever seen in his life. It wasn't over quickly either. They kissed like it was nowhere near the first time. Salem's entire body was sweating. His jaw was practically on the floor. Nothing could have shocked him more.

Quest pulled away, and the pair acted like nothing happened.

Dodge drew a card.

Salem held up a hand. "Hold up. What the hell was that?"

Two faces innocently stared at him.

Quest shrugged. "I don't know what you mean."

Salem motioned between them, completely stunned and unable to shake it. "That. You kissed him."

Sexy chuckles rumbled from Quest and Dodge. Dodge's smile turned wicked as hell. "I mean, yeah. You know we're always down for anything."

"But you're straight." Salem didn't know why he couldn't stop arguing. He had seen what he had seen.

Both men blinked at him. "Says who?" Quest finally said, breaking the silence.

That was a fair question. Yet Salem couldn't stop. "Says me. I never seen either of you bring home a guy. Always only women."

"Bi erasure."

At Dodge's sad-sounding comment, Salem almost blew his lid. "What the fuck? I call bullshit. Exactly how many guys have you slept with, then?" Salem knew he sounded crazy, but he couldn't stop. They were straight. They had to be.

The pair exchanged a look and answered simultaneously. "One."

Salem's brain ceased working. They didn't have to explain any further. He got it. They meant each other. It was always them. He felt... Salem wasn't sure how he felt. Hurt, if he was being honest. Like they had kept something from him.

Dodge read his card while Salem reeled. "Ask your dad how old he was the first time he fucked your mom or suck the player to your left's neck. Dad is dead, so..."

With Salem still sunk in his feelings, he didn't fully listen. Then Dodge snagged the back of his head and hauled Salem forward. He nuzzled Salem's neck for a moment before his mouth opened. Dodge sucked.

Salem moaned. God help him. The sound escaped and there was noth-ing he could do. Then a solid chest pressed against his back. Fingers buried in Salem's hair and pulled his head back. A mouth covered his. In some sort of wild, detached way, Salem understood Quest kissed him while Dodge found his way beneath Salem's t-shirt to lick his nipple. Not once had Salem been so knocked senseless. His soul wanted what it wanted. It had denied this love and lust for too long.

Quest tore his mouth away and urged him toward Dodge. Like that, Dodge's tongue filled his mouth. He had no idea how much time passed or any-thing happening outside the hands on his body. His pajama pants slid down his hips. Salem didn't even know who divested him of them.

All he knew was clothes disappeared and Salem couldn't resist kissing his way down Dodge's amazing chest and abs. The moment his bottom lip hit Dodge's bare erection, Salem knew it was over. That was the point of no return. He swallowed Dodge's dick while Quest kissed his spine. The sounds Dodge made kept him going even as wet fingers stretched his asshole. He wanted to see them. To watch them as they came. Salem knew it would be the most beautiful sight of his life.

Something much bigger pressed against the tight ring of muscles surrounding his asshole. He couldn't say no. Just one time. They couldn't do this again after tonight. Salem hadn't exaggerated earlier. Losing them was his biggest nightmare. They had each other. Salem had no one. Just the thought nearly had him panicking. Then Quest pushed his way inside and Salem forgot to care. He wasn't alone tonight. Salem moaned around Dodge's cock. Dodge gasped. "Salem." The way Dodge whispered his name made goosebumps rise on Salem's skin. There was reverence mixed with love. Tears filled Salem's eyes. He wished more times than he could count that he had the words. Quest's lips touched his shoulder as he pumped inside Salem. Salem broke at the touch. They were too much.

The tears dropped, hitting Dodge's skin.

Dodge grabbed his hair and yanked, forcing Salem to meet his stare. He looked devastated at the sight of Salem's tears. Salem's heart squeezed. He would never want them to hurt.

"I don't want to stop."

Dodge still didn't release his hair at the confession. His gaze moved over Salem's face. Salem saw all the questions he couldn't answer.

"I don't want to stop," Salem repeated. This time, he ensured Dodge heard the lust in his voice.

Dodge stroked his face. "I can't watch you hurt."

Salem took his hand and gently set it away. "It's not pain you're seeing."

Dodge nodded.

Salem held his stare as he lowered his head and licked Dodge's cock. Quest's sexy muscular arm appeared in the corner of his vision as he braced his weight as he kissed Salem's ear.

"You feel every bit as amazing as I knew you would. It's taking everything I have not to blow and disappoint you. But you can still say no, beautiful. It's never too late, okay?

You matter too much to us. We couldn't hurt you."

"You're both wanted." Salem moaned as Quest rocked inside him at the perfect angle when the words left his lips. "You have no fucking idea how badly you're wanted." Salem sucked Dodge, needing him to feel as good as they made him feel every day. He also needed his mouth to do something other than confess his secrets. This was the one thing he would never have. Just one night.

Quest set to work, and Salem did too. The closer he got to the edge, the more Salem threw at Dodge. The way Dodge gasped, moaned, and rambled incoherently fucked with

Salem's head and added to his pleasure.

Salem grabbed a handful of covers and held tightly as he wound tighter and tighter. Cum filled his mouth. Cries assaulted his ears. Salem flew apart. Cum ran down Dodge's erection. Salem was too far gone to swallow. All he could focus on was the way his body jerked and twitched. Pleasure rocked his soul. His arms shook. They wanted to give out under the assault on his senses.

Quest's lips touched his ear again. A chuckle vibrated against its shell. "None of that, now. We're nowhere near finished with you."

Salem's head spun. He had promised himself only one night. The night wasn't over yet. He would take as much as his body allowed. No regrets and then never again.

CHAPTER THREE

JUST THE SOUND OF Salem's breathing steadied Dodge. He understood
now why Quest always said Dodge
soothed him. The peace he found
with the two men who slept nearby couldn't be understated. Before JD
had come into his life, Dodge hadn't
known this stillness. There was no
way Quest and Salem understood
how tired he got of smoking to find
what they brought him. He had to
find a way to hang on to this, but

he had never been good at asking for what he wanted. Rejection was more than he could handle on the best of days. If either Salem or Quest ever turned their back on him, he couldn't survive it. Dodge was already barely hanging on mentally.

Salem stirred.

Dodge pretended to sleep, hoping to hang on to the moment for a second longer. When he felt Salem stiffen, he knew their moment was gone. Salem slithered down the bed, sneaking his way from between them. Despite Salem leaving him, Dodge fought a smile at the way Salem worked at not waking them. Dodge didn't open his eyes until he was certain Salem was gone. Quest slept peacefully. Dodge waited five minutes before following Salem.

He slipped into Salem's bedroom just in time to catch Salem getting into the shower. It was a risk, but Dodge had to take it. He couldn't let Salem cool too long or think too much. Otherwise, he was out. Dodge felt Salem's fear all hours of the day, like a fourth person living in their home. Of course, to be fair, that fourth person had been created by all of them. But Dodge needed this. He couldn't run now.

Dodge opened the shower door and stepped inside. Salem didn't startle. That was Salem, though. He was the most solid person Dodge had ever met. His spine of steel never bent. The only time he ever softened was with them. That was why Dodge knew he had made the right choice.

Salem's expression was heat and curiosity.

Dodge didn't make him ask. "I didn't get to do what I really wanted last night." He lifted Salem off his feet and backed him against the wall. "Not that I'm complaining."

A smile exploded across Salem's face. He stroked the back of Dodge's neck—the way he always did. "It's not in you to bitch about anything, but I get what you're saying."

God. Dodge loved him. He couldn't stop smiling. "I guess this didn't turn out that sexy."

"Sometimes, sexy is overrated. Real is better."

Dodge pressed his forehead against Salem's for a moment. They held each other's stare. Salem made the first move. He pressed his lips against Dodge's. Dodge savored the feeling of touching Salem before deepening their kiss. Things got hotter by the second, even though Dodge was woefully unprepared to take this shot. "Show me."

Salem grabbed a nearby bottle that looked like some sort of oil. "Sit down. I've got you."

Dodge carefully sat on the bench inside the wet room. On his knees, straddling Dodge's lap, Salem used the oil on his asshole while Dodge watched. He was painfully turned on. Dodge had religiously worn protection his entire life. It was Salem. Not only had Dodge not been with anyone in a while, his soul knew they were meant to be. Salem didn't see it yet, but this was where they all stopped—together.

Still, not having Quest there to shore up his mental health kept fucking with his head. "Sorry, I'm not Quest. I know he's the one with all the skills."

Salem froze. His steely gaze locked on to Dodge. "Stop. Don't do that." Salem set the oil aside and scooted closer, removing the space between them. He wrapped his arms around Dodge's neck. Salem never broke eye contact, and Dodge couldn't look away. "You have the most gentle, loving soul I've ever seen. Quest is the 'everyone gets love in this house' one. He's not better or vice versa. Just different. Do you think he's better than me?" Salem lifted and took Dodge inside him. Everything inside Dodge glitched to the point he couldn't respond. Salem rocked himself on

Dodge's cock and kept going. "Do you think I'm better than him?"

"You're different." The words stuttered from Dodge's lips.

Salem swiped his lips across Dodge's mouth. "Exactly. This isn't a competition. It's three pieces of one soul finding each other."

Goddamn. Dodge flew to his feet, holding Salem's weight. He braced him against the wall and fucked him the way he had always wanted. Dodge didn't think. He acted. Even though it was Salem, he became the person who fucked anyone else. Dodge took his pleasure while following Salem's cues. If he moaned,

Dodge leaned into that angle. Everything felt good to him. He couldn't be disappointed, but he also knew he wouldn't let Salem down. Salem believed in him and loved him. That was all he needed to let go and enjoy their time. When Salem's cum hit his chest, a roar of possessiveness and satisfaction filled his head.

The way Salem's body felt—the heat. The way he tried sucking him deeper. Dodge had never experienced anything so powerful. He knew that was because his heart was all the way in, but the ecstasy nearly unglued his mind. He chanted Salem's name against his throat as he filled Salem with cum. It felt like a claiming, but

Dodge knew it wasn't. Salem still held something back from him. He felt it all hours of the day. There was some part of Salem they couldn't reach. Until they did, Salem would never agree to be theirs.

With a towel wrapped around his waist, Quest ambled from the bathroom into the bedroom. He found Dodge nude on his knees, picking up the box of cards that had spilled everywhere during last night's encounter.

"I planned to do that when I got out of the shower."

Dodge looked up. His sweet, hazel eyes locked on to Quest. Quest's heart skipped a beat. Dodge smiled. "Hey. It's no big deal. I came in here to get it."

Quest's gaze swept Dodge's nude body. "Is that what you came here to do?"

Dodge blushed. "I was on my way to my bedroom. I forgot to get dressed." Quest's heart had never stood a chance. Not from day one.

Quest plopped down on the bed and stretched out. He opened his arms to Dodge.

With a huge grin, Dodge crawled into Quest's embrace. He snuggled against Quest's chest.

Quest took a deep breath. "You smell like him—like whatever product he uses or whatever. You know what I mean."

"I think we pushed too hard, too fast. He left. Practically ran from the house."

He wasn't surprised. "I think three years is a long enough wait. It'll be okay."

"He cried. Last night," Dodge explained unnecessarily. Quest had been there.

"You remember what it was like. When no one has ever loved you, it's hard. He's not like us. For someone like him, this whole thing will be even harder to swallow."

Silence stretched between them.

Dodge cleared his throat. "This whole thing. What is that exactly?"

God. Quest had been waiting for Dodge to ask that for a long time. He knew Dodge had to come to him. Too much had happened to Dodge. His incredibly sweet nature had been more than abused. Dodge had to be the one to choose. "It's always been us, babe. I've just been waiting for you to be done with playing. You're owed that freedom."

Dodge shifted, as if getting more comfortable. "One morning, like three months after Dad died, we woke up and Salem had cooked breakfast. I know he's always done that, but it just hit me from nowhere. He made this a home. I mean, I get that JD indulged us, but this was different. Salem glued us together. I know I don't make sense."

A lump grew in Quest's throat. "You make perfect sense. JD loved us, but his love language was money. It's like we needed a steadiness or something like that." He chuckled. "I guess I'm the one who doesn't make sense now."

Dodge's hand moved across Quest's stomach, stroking him. "Nah. I get you, but I forgot my point. That's the day I knew I wanted it to be just us. The three of us." He plucked at Quest's towel nervously. Dodge cleared his throat again. Quest practically felt how uncomfortable this conversation was for him. "It's been really hard watching you both choose everyone but me."

Quest rolled, pinning Dodge beneath him. Dodge looked every bit as vulnerable as he sounded. "I'd never choose anyone over you. Why in the fuck do you think I drink so much? I fucking hate seeing Salem and you choosing everyone but me. From day one, I was more than willing to be only yours."

Dodge looked sad rather than reassured. "I just thought you didn't want me anymore."

"How could you think I don't want you?" Quest shifted positions, ensuring Dodge couldn't miss his erection. Even Quest heard the rage in his voice. Quest realized he had lost his towel in the fracas when it sank in there was nothing between them.

Dodge stroked his ass. "I love you."

Quest softened immediately. He couldn't explain it, but he loved the sound of Dodge's voice. His shoulders relaxed at just the sound, much less while saying those words with their nude bodies molded together. "I love you too. Seriously, though. How could you think I don't want you?"

The sweetest shrug came from beneath him. He watched Dodge turn adorably shy. Quest knew most people never saw the real Dodge. They saw an overly confident beauty. It was a facade. While Dodge was definitely flawless, he was still the same painfully broken boy Quest met nearly a decade ago. He counted on Quest. "Like Salem pointed out last night, you never dated any other men. I thought... well, you know what I thought."

He did, and it broke his heart. Quest lowered his head and kissed Dodge, lightly swiping his lips across Dodge's before moving to kiss his cheek. "I more than want you. I want it to be just us. The three of us, exactly as fate intended." He licked Dodge's collarbone. "I'm sorry I've failed you. Tell me how I can fix it?" He sucked Dodge's nipple, listening to the way his breathing turned ragged. Quest softened his voice even more, luring Dodge from the shell he hid in when he was embarrassed to talk about something. "Tell me how I could've made you see the way I die a little each night you're not sleeping beside me."

Dodge snagged his hair and pulled, dragging Quest's mouth back to his. He dove inside. His tongue fought Quest for control. Quest's throat swelled even as his hips automatically rolled. Their erections enjoyed the friction while their mouths played. Everything in Quest's chest hurt even as his body burned. His eyes stung. He wanted this life so goddamn badly and it was like he was invisible. Quest tried so hard to give this household all the love he had, and he swore no one noticed how badly he needed to be loved too.

Dodge swiped Quest's face. "Why in the fuck are you crying? Why am I making everyone cry?"

He sounded so adorably confused and hurt. Quest chuckled. "They're tears of happiness." He kissed Dodge's neck, trying to hide his expression. Quest was horrified. He hadn't realized he was crying. Quest was supposed to be the older one. The stronger one. He rocked against Dodge again. Quest had to distract him. "You have no idea how much I've missed this." He kept up the pace, savoring the friction. "You have no idea how many women I've chosen, only because I knew you'd share them with me. Just so I could be closer to you. You and Salem are my whole fucking world. I just haven't known how to make you two see me."

Dodge grabbed his hair again, forcing Quest to hold his stare as he lifted his hips and did his part to drive Quest crazy. He never looked away. Quest's stomach muscles clenched. He was turned on and invested. Quest needed this. "I see you. It's me I've never been able to look at too closely."

Damn. That crushed Quest. He had known that, but he had been too scared of his own feelings and losing what they had built in this house to give Dodge what he needed. "I see you just fine and I promise you all there is to look at is pure beauty. Not just on the outside. Inside, where it matters, you're so fucking stunning. You leave me speechless. Always have."

Using his strength against Quest, Dodge rolled. Dodge held their erections together and stroked. He kissed Quest like he wanted to consume him. Quest's lust won. All talks of their past and relationship ended. Quest writhed against Dodge's touch, riding his palm while savoring the way their erections felt against each other. There was so much love in his heart. Sometimes it had nowhere to go. His body wound tighter. Quest's breathing turned more ragged. He fought his way toward the pleasure Dodge offered. Dodge didn't tease. He worked and used Quest's body like he couldn't spit cum on him fast enough. His kiss showed a hunger that matched the way Quest starved.

Dodge cried out against Quest's lips.

Quest lost his breath as the show of Dodge's orgasm took him out. His body jerked when Dodge's hot cum spilled over his crown. Then there was nothing but the ecstasy of pulsations that had him fucking Dodge's hand, refusing to miss a single wave. This was love. Always had been. How could Salem resist them now that they knew exactly what they sought? They would be so fucking flawless.

CHAPTER FOUR

WHEN SALEM HAD SHOWN up at Tarek's door before his scheduled lunch date with Shaw, he hadn't known what he sought exactly. After two glasses of wine, his shoulders relaxed, but his tongue refused. Salem never knew how to talk about the things that mattered to him. He could be there for anyone and everyone else, but he had no idea how to be weak enough to be vulnerable.

"So... date number two with Shaw. That must be a record for you since JD passed. Sounds like you might actually like someone."

Salem nodded. He started to say Shaw was stimulating. That wasn't what happened. "Actually, I kind of ended up getting spit-roasted by Quest and Dodge last night. Then I had sex with Dodge in the shower this morning." The confession burst from him, so deadpan and lifeless, that Tarek laughed.

A second passed and Tarek's laughter died. "Wait. You're serious."

"Unfortunately."

Tarek's brow furrowed. "Why unfortunately? They're both gorgeous, and the three of you have an amazing relationship."

Salem tried to soften his tone so he didn't sound like a lifeless robot. He couldn't. "They're JD's sons."

"Stepsons," Tarek reminded him with a huff. "Former stepsons, at that. By two different wives. Both of which he was no longer married to by his death, obviously. All of that you know better than anyone, so be for real. Why are you upset?"

Fuck. Tarek knew he was upset. Salem had to fix that. He forced his shoulders to relax. "The three of us live together. They're my people. Introducing sex can only destroy what we've built. But I can't un–ring that bell, so I don't know."

Tarek blinked. "Did you actually come to me for advice? There's no way Salem Rochester doesn't know how to take control of a situation."

Salem relaxed for real. Tarek was right. He would never give up enough control to anyone for this situation to be anything but handled. "You're right. Thank you."

Tarek blinked again and then again, obviously confused as hell. "I mean, okay. You're welcome, I guess."

Salem's gaze moved over Tarek's stylishly mussed dark hair and dark-ly lined eyes. He truly was a beauty. It had been easy to position Tarek into a comfortable life with an older man who worshiped the ground he walked on. He was Salem's friend. Salem loved him. Tarek knew him almost as well as Quest and Dodge. If Tarek thought he could iron will his way out of this situation, then Salem could. This was why he had come here. His subconscious had known what to do and where to go.

Salem breathed easier. "Tell me about your life."

Another loud laugh burst from Tarek. "Um. Okay. If you absolutely refuse to give me every juicy detail about last night, then I guess I don't have a choice. Portland is making noises about early retirement and us enjoying a quiet life."

"How do you feel about that?" Salem had to focus on someone else.

"Whatever makes him happy makes me happy. Seriously, Salem. You can talk to me about things."

Salem nodded. "All right. I've already accepted a third date with Shaw."

Tarek huffed. "I know. He called me after your coffee date the other day. How do Dodge and Quest feel about last night? Do they think this is some-

thing casual everyone can forget hap–
pened?"

"It's a society dinner."

That seemed to distract Tarek from
Salem's bad decisions. "Wait. Really?
You're stepping foot back into society?
Shaw didn't tell me that."

"I'm sure he doesn't realize how
against the community of arrogant
bastards I am, but yes. It seems I'm
stepping back into the vipers' nest.
Better that firing squad than the one
at home."

"Wow." Tarek sat back, sinking into
his expensive and comfy couch. He
took a sip of wine while staring into

space. "Wow," he repeated after a moment. "That's..."

Yeah. Salem knew. It would be vicious. He would be miserable. It was a mistake. They would do their damnedest to eat him alive. Apparently, Salem had been feeling destructive lately.

Portland strolled into the room, looking as deadly as ever. Of course, he softened the minute he kissed Tarek. Salem openly watched, wishing he knew how to bend the way Portland did. Blue eyes finally swung his way. "Salem. It's nice to see you."

Salem dipped his chin. "You as well. Sorry for dropping by without calling. I didn't realize you planned to come home early. I'd never interrupt a newlywed couple's time."

Portland snorted and dropped into the spot next to Tarek on the couch. He tucked Tarek against his side. "You're allowed to drop by whenever you want. I've just been having a harder time staying away lately. My schedule keeps getting shorter. Today, I kept things to one morning meeting. In fact, I'm thinking of retiring."

"That's what Tarek was just telling me." Salem checked his watch. He felt a little too exposed today. "I guess I should head out if I intend to get to Shaw's office on time."

Portland smiled. "Date number two. Shaw must be doing something right."

It took everything Salem possessed not to look Tarek's way. "He hasn't bored me, but the day is young."

A bark of laughter burst from Portland. "Try not to wreck him too badly."

Salem genuinely liked Portland. Despite being a drug lord, he had that steel inside him that always appealed to Salem. "I feel certain he'll survive it. His head is pretty big."

"A match made in heaven," Portland said with a chuckle.

Salem stood. "Or hell. We'll see which soon enough, I'm sure." He saw the way Tarek fought not to talk about Quest and Dodge. Salem had to get out of there.

Salem stood.

Tarek bounded to his feet. "I'll walk you to the door."

Fuck. "That's not necessary."

Tarek linked arms with him. "Sure it is. I have to get my hugs." He practically dragged Salem to the door. Tarek barely made it out of earshot. "Please think about giving the boys a real shot. They love you. You love them. I'd hate for you three to miss something beautiful. Just give it some thought," Tarek said before Salem could argue.

Instead of bothering to admit that was all he ever thought about, Salem kissed Tarek's cheek and hugged him. "I love you. Go enjoy your husband. Being cherished is rarer than you think." He barely heard Tarek returning his "I love you" before he was out the door. Behind the wheel of his Audi, Salem took a few steadying breaths before pulling away. There was no avoiding an early arrival to Shaw's office unless he found something else to do. Salem didn't need to be alone with his thoughts. His mind could be a dangerous place.

Still, when Salem arrived at Howe's Law Offices, he sat for a minute before climbing from the car. The last thing he wanted was to seem too eager. He had a bad feeling everyone would get hurt before the end. Salem wished he hadn't let his guard down. He owned toys. It wasn't like he couldn't take care of his own needs. Why in the fuck had he even let himself start thinking about being touched again? Nothing good ever came from him wanting things.

Salem hardened himself. This was lunch. He would keep their plans because he didn't flake on people. Salem would also keep his plans to join Shaw at a society banquet. No one wanted to go to those things alone. Beyond that, he would pull back. He wouldn't give Shaw any ideas. Salem hadn't quite decided how he would rebuild the wall between the boys and him, but he would. Some people weren't meant to have what Tarek had with Portland. People like Salem were better off if no one saw what was beneath the shell.

With shoulders squared, Salem headed for the door. He strolled inside like he belonged—the way he did everywhere he went. Salem was not the poor Louisiana boy with the tattered clothes and dirty hair. He had crawled his way from that version of himself and now was one of the richest men in America. It mattered not at all what anyone thought of him now. He could buy the haters.

"For fuck's sake, Joesph. I gave you one job today and you couldn't even do that."

"And seventy-five yesterday. Fifty the day before that. How do you think shit gets done while you're out having lunch dates and chatting with your little buddies? It's me. I'm here pulling your fucking weight."

Salem froze in the doorway. He had no desire to step into the middle of Shaw's very loud argument with the mouthy employee. To Salem's surprise, the pissed-off guy going toe to toe with Shaw rolled from behind the desk and wheeled his chair across the room. He disappeared into an office and came back out with a small box of stuff on his lap.

"All your shit was already in a box?"

"Goddamn right. No one should have to put up with the shit I do from you. Go play with your friend." He motioned toward the door. "Let him think you're important with all your bought and paid for judges, while I'm the one who actually does your fucking job."

Salem jumped out of the man's way as he awkwardly shoved his way through the door, banging his wheel-chair on everything as he went.

"Would you like—" The question died on Salem's lips as rage-filled light blue eyes swung his way. Salem held his hands up and backed away, minding his business.

"Joesph." Shaw sounded so defeated.

"Go fuck yourself, Shaw."

Shaw pinched the spot between his eyes.

Salem waited until they were alone to speak. "It looks like you could use a rain check on that lunch."

A woman at a corner desk tried to pretend she didn't exist.

Shaw dropped his hand and released a loud sigh. "No. It's fine." He focused on what Salem assumed was his receptionist. "Please forward any emergencies."

"Yes, sir."

It was rare for Salem to be uncomfortable, but he hated conflict. He didn't mind a good word–sparring match, but actual contention was too much. One reason he had been so content with JD had been the peace. He could sit in total silence for the rest of his life and be fine. His life had been so goddamn loud.

Salem shifted from foot to foot. "Are you sure you're good to leave?"

"I said I was fine!"

Salem jumped at the barked words. Then his spine stiffened. "Good. Enjoy your lunch." He strolled right back out the same door he had just entered.

He didn't make it to his car before Shaw overcame him. Shaw was in his space, blocking his way to his car before Salem could make a clean break. "I'm sorry. This has been a terrible morning. I shouldn't have snapped at you. You didn't deserve that."

Salem drew a steadying breath. He had to admit Shaw seemed genuinely apologetic, but abusers always were. Salem managed a small smile. It was best to be polite and fade away. "I appreciate your apology, but you truly have your hands full and I..."

"Won't be yelled at by some guy you just met," Shaw finished for him. "I get it. No one knows better than me how bad of a first impression I've made with you."

Damn. He was smooth. Salem didn't know what to think. "I think it's just bad timing. Maybe another time."

Shaw crowded his space. Salem didn't know why he didn't step back, but his feet simply didn't move. Shaw rubbed Salem's arms, almost as if trying to warm him. Salem didn't realize until he focused on the gesture how badly he shook. He fucking hated that. Salem locked his back teeth, trying to force his body to obey.

A sexy, dark green gaze moved over his face. "I'm okay with postponing this, but I'm not okay with you leaving here thinking I'd ever hurt you. Sometimes I get loud and intolerable." Shaw smiled, looking contrite. "It's my job. I'm argumentative and stubborn. There's nothing I hate more than to lose. Joesph is the same and we drive each other nuts. A lot."

Despite himself, Salem smiled at Shaw's not bothering to pretend it was only a little. "Are you sure you don't want to go try to win back your..." Salem had no idea what Joesph did. "Joesph back?"

"I should probably let him cool down first. He likely owns a gun."

A laugh fell from Salem's lips and he knew Shaw had won. "Okay. I guess I can't let you get shot. Let's get you something to eat so you're not facing him hangry."

To Shaw's credit, he didn't look overly triumphant. "Good idea." With the ease of a master, Shaw swept him toward a nearby luxury car. Salem wasn't a car guy, so he didn't recognize the brand, but he was a money guy, so he knew expensive when he saw it. Shaw hadn't quite lost his attention yet. Maybe, if nothing else, they could be friends.

Dodge couldn't recall the last time he felt so much at peace. While he knew things weren't settled or set in stone, he didn't feel like everything slowly slipped away. The way he had for a long time now. He had hoped Salem would come home in time for lunch, but he refused to dampen the day by overthinking it when he didn't. Instead, Quest offered to take him to their favorite restaurant. Quest held the door open for him and Dodge had to squelch an idiotic smile. It wasn't often he got to feel like someone took care of him. He was usually the one opening doors.

The place was slammed. Crowd size didn't matter. Dodge spotted Salem with Shaw like Salem had magnetized his eyes. He drew Quest close and nodded toward the table where the pair sat across from one another. There were four chairs. Two were empty.

"Two?"

Quest looked the hostess' way. "Our party is right there." He motioned toward Salem.

With a smile, the woman grabbed two menus and led them to Salem's table. Dodge didn't hesitate to grab a chair and sit, interrupting a date Salem had a lot of goddamn nerve to be on.

Annoyance flashed in Shaw's eyes. He was smart enough to quickly mask it.

A smile exploded across Salem's face, easing the pressure in Dodge's chest. "Hey, guys. Where did you two come from?"

Dodge answered as he scooted in. "Home."

Quest visibly bit back a laugh. He knew Dodge too well. Dodge often leaned into people, thinking he was dumb. That was the label the upper crust community had given him a long time ago. So, fuck people like Shaw. He knew he wasn't Ivy League or anything, but goddamn. Dodge didn't eat glue.

"We didn't expect to see you here, but wow. This place is slammed today."

Salem nodded at Quest's words. "We were surprised too. Apparently, there's some sort of convention in town. You probably would've had to wait over an hour if we didn't have extra seats."

Dodge gave a sharp nod, satisfied by Salem's willingness to accept their gate crashing.

Quest didn't seem as easily appeased. "Still, imagine our surprise." He held Salem's stare.

Dodge decided he had better distract Shaw. "How long did you two have to wait?"

Dark green eyes focused on him. "Not long. We had reservations."

Damn. This was a planned date. "Smart." Hands landed on his shoulders. "Excuse me. Sorry." Dodge scooted his chair closer to the table, making room for the woman to pass.

Salem snorted.

"Whole goddamn football field back there," Quest muttered under his breath.

Dodge looked around the table, trying to figure out what he missed. Salem and Quest were exchanging a knowing glance while Shaw had death daggers in his eyes as he stared across the room. Dodge followed his gaze. A guy in a wheelchair sat with another man at a table, seemingly oblivious to Shaw murdering them with his stare.

"Do you have something against disabled people?"

Shaw blinked at Dodge's question and tore his gaze away from the pair. "What sort of idiotic question is that?"

"Whoa." Quest was obviously ready to square up at Shaw's words.

Dodge was used to it, and he had been baiting him.

Salem was already scooting his chair back. "I can't believe I fell for that apology."

Dodge ignored it all. "I was only asking because of the way you were trying to kill that guy with your eyes."

Salem looked over his shoulder. "Oh. It's Joesph. They had a fight earlier."

A muscle ticked in Quest's jaw.

Dodge decided it was time to defuse the situation. "That was on me. I shouldn't have assumed something like that about your character. Sorry, man."

Shaw looked Salem's way. It was obvious his decision to accept Dodge's apology rode on if Salem left.

Salem didn't scoot back toward the table, but he no longer looked angry. "Should we go somewhere else? You just calmed down."

Shaw's shoulders visibly relaxed. His smile turned genuine. "It's fine. I'm over it. Let's just enjoy lunch." He focused on Dodge. "It's okay. I get the feeling you're someone who calls out injustices. That's admirable, even if it was directed at me."

Oh no. He was smooth. Dodge didn't know if he could compete with that. He looked Quest's way. The same muscle still jumped in his jaw, but he stared at the menu.

A beer appeared in front of him. "This is from that lady at the bar."

Salem laughed and looked toward where the server indicated.

Quest sighed.

A low chuckle rumbled from Shaw.

Dodge blinked at the glass. "Oh. Okay. Uh, thanks, I guess." He didn't bother looking toward the bar. Having a drink delivered to someone was weird. He pushed the glass toward Quest.

"Dodge doesn't drink," Salem explained.

Quest pushed the glass Shaw's way. "I'm cutting back."

Shaw glanced at the glass. "I'm technically working today."

"For fuck's sake." Salem snatched up the drink and headed for the bar.

Dodge watched in horror as he carried the beer to a woman in a red top and black leggings. She was blonde and pretty, but he wasn't interested. Salem spoke to her, wearing all smiles before returning empty-handed. "There. She's really sorry for the misunderstanding. Is everyone satisfied?"

Not really. Now he felt bad.

Obviously reading his mind, Salem stroked his arm. "It's okay, puppy. She wasn't upset. I'm superb at rejecting people."

Shaw snorted, but wasn't dumb enough to speak.

The muscle in Quest's jaw worked double time.

Dodge really wished he felt better.

Quest stood. "Come on, Dodge. We're obviously interrupting a date. Let's go to The Three-Legged Cowboy instead. I noticed they had a menu taped by the door and we got a lot of interesting offers last night."

Whoa. Quest was for real pissed and would make a scene if Dodge didn't leave with him.

Shaw looked amused.

Salem stared at his menu like his life depended on it, but there was no missing the way his shoulders were set—the way they always were when he tried to hold himself together.

"Okay. Sorry, guys. I didn't realize." He stood and pushed in his chair. Without looking back or waiting for a response, Dodge followed Quest to the door. He rushed ahead and held open the door for Quest, hoping to smooth things over. Dodge wasn't sure exactly what he had done wrong, but it definitely felt like his fault. The second he heard the doors unlock on Quest's truck, he ran to open that door for Quest as well.

Instead of climbing inside, Quest snagged Dodge's waist and swept him inside the open doorway. The tall vehicle somewhat hid them from sight. Quest's mouth covered his. Their tongues battled. The quivering inside Dodge eased. He didn't feel quite as much tightness in his chest.

Quest pulled away and kissed his cheek. "I'm sorry. Let's just run through the drive-thru somewhere. I didn't mean to ruin lunch."

"Okay."

Quest didn't release him. He held Dodge's stare. His heart was in his eyes. "I love you. I just can't sit there with that bastard."

Dodge nodded. "Okay. I love you too."

"Really, I'm sorry. I didn't mean to embarrass you."

"How did you embarrass me?" Dodge was confused as hell.

Quest swiped a hand over his eyes. "That whole Three-Legged Cowboy thing and claiming people offered us a bunch of shit. Jesus. I don't know what happened."

Dodge cupped Quest's face between his hands so he couldn't get away. "Stop. I'm not embarrassed. If you think I care if people think I'm gay, you should know I don't. If you think I don't want anyone to know we're more than ex–stepbrothers, that's bullshit. I love you. I'll never be ashamed of that. Okay?"

Quest nodded. He looked devastated. Dodge got it. Quest hated losing his temper, even more so when Salem was around. Salem couldn't handle other people's anger.

Dodge kissed him. "It's okay. You didn't do anything wrong."

Quest nodded again.

Love swelled inside Dodge's chest. He saw how hard Quest fought to hold everything and everyone together. He had to feel like no one did the same for him. "Get in. I'm driving. I have an idea."

With another defeated-looking nod, Quest circled the truck and climbed inside. Dodge filled the driver's seat and waited until Quest had his seatbelt on to pull from the lot. Sometimes, knowing someone for a long time paid off. Dodge knew exactly how to fix this.

Defeat sat heavily on Quest's shoulders. From the moment he saw Salem with someone else, rage coated his vision. Then Shaw had called Dodge an idiot. Someone else had blatantly hit on Dodge. Salem didn't leave with them. Everything felt like a fucking mess. He had no idea where they were headed. Quest didn't even pay attention to his surroundings. All he saw was the dozen ways he had fucked up today.

Then Dodge pulled into the parking lot of a mini golf course that was owned by one of the biggest gossips in town. They had come here a lot back when Dodge first came to live with him. Then the owner had kept spreading rumors about Dodge among the upper crust. They had all been true, but that was another story, and a huge part of Dodge's mental destruction. Until then, though, Quest had loved this place. It was loud and bright. Fun. It reminded him of Dodge's personality when he was happy—like when they worked on creating a new game. Dodge could be so animated. Mesmerizing.

"Come on." Dodge climbed from the truck before Quest could remind him who owned the place.

Quest reluctantly slipped from the vehicle. He barely made it two steps before Dodge was at his side, holding his hand. He dragged Quest toward the door.

"What are we doing?"

Dodge flashed him a smile so blinding, it stunned him into silence. He forgot what they were talking about. "Just trust me."

"I do."

Inside, in the semidarkness, arcade games flashed and played various competing sounds. Quest never knew where to look first.

"This way."

It wasn't like he had a choice. Dodge still held his hand.

"Two for course one, please?"

Quest awkwardly accepted the club he was handed, and he picked a yellow ball. Even once they were outside, his head didn't clear. Still, he placed his ball at the first hole and swung. He hit it too hard. "Damn. I'm rusty. It's been a while."

"I know. Go get your ball and try again. That one doesn't count. Call it a practice swing."

With a smile, Quest jogged to get his ball and came back. The happiness in Dodge's expression was contagious.

Dodge never let him stay down for long.

Before he got set up to swing again, Dodge crowded his space, pressing against his back. He wrapped his arms around Quest. His lips brushed Quest's ear. "You just need the right pressure." He helped Quest swing. Quest didn't even see what happened to the ball. He was turned on and blind to everything except Dodge. Then Dodge didn't let up. Hole by hole, he touched Quest. Kissed him. His gaze fucked him. The air felt too thin. Everything had a haze to it. It was like the only thing clear in his eyes was Dodge. Maybe his beauty simply outshined the rest of the world. Quest couldn't say anymore.

At the eighteenth hole, Quest tried to focus. The game was almost over and he could end this torture. He moved to hit his ball. Dodge stepped into his path, blocking him. Without warning, his mouth covered Quest's in a kiss so carnal, Quest nearly came right then.

Dodge pulled away and swiped the moisture from Quest's bottom lip with his thumb. His gaze never wavered from holding Quest's stare. "Let them spread that rumor. It's long past time for everyone to know you're mine and they can't have you."

Quest had never felt weaker in his life, or stronger. There was nothing he wouldn't give this man, and he would tear apart the world if anyone tried to harm him. He had been drowning in love since they met. Dodge was right. It was time everyone knew.

Chapter Five

Salem didn't hear the chirp of the alarm from the back door opening until he pulled the last dish from the oven. The scent of food filled the kitchen. He didn't doubt they smelled the steak he had just fetched from the grill. The pair ambled into the room. Salem felt their overwhelming presence, but he didn't turn. He simply seasoned the chopped potatoes and stayed focused on his task.

"Something smells good."

Salem's eyes fell closed. He wanted to cry, but he wouldn't. From the very beginning, he had known he was the third wheel. The outsider. He hadn't had any illusions about them. They would always choose each other first and Salem last. He didn't doubt they had spent the day fucking whoever it was they picked up from the bar. It was Salem's fault. He was cold. That was life.

He swallowed the hurt. "You're just in time. I just finished. No doubt you worked up an appetite today." Salem might have bitten off his tongue if he hadn't managed to cling to a bland tone. They could have his heart, but Salem would keep his pride.

He found himself squashed between two massive bodies. With a spatula in one hand and salt in the other, Salem stood like an awkward statue while they squeezed him. They didn't smell like sex. They smelled like sunshine.

"You missed mini golf."

"And then real golf," Dodge tacked on, finishing Quest's claim.

"I don't enjoy either of those things, so I'm good."

"Are you good?"

At Quest's question, Salem wanted to scream at the top of his lungs. No. He wasn't okay. Salem hated absolutely everyone, and he never had anywhere to go with that.

"I had already said I'd go to lunch with Shaw and join him for a society banquet before last night. I'd never hurt either of you. It truly was just lunch. We didn't even shake hands when it was over." Salem had no idea why he explained himself. They had each other. He meant nothing.

"Stop talking, Salem."

Salem's teeth snapped together at Quest's demand.

"Is everything turned off—like the stove and whatnot?"

Salem nodded.

The world tilted. He ended up draped over Quest's shoulder.

While smiling like an idiot, Dodge plucked the items from his hands and set them aside. "I'll make our plates."

Salem had no idea what was happening. They were both bad about using their size against him. Quest could have anything planned. He fought the urge to laugh when Quest paced a circle around the kitchen island. Then Quest started talking, and he fought not to panic.

"Listen up, gorgeous. We're not doing this. You're not gonna pretend like last night didn't happen." Quest kept pacing his circle while he spoke. "If you want to freak out or be angry with us, then do it, but don't treat us like we're toys you can use and set aside when you're done. We are people. We have feelings and we care about your feelings. You're not allowed to shut us out. You're supposed to love us. At least that's what you've claimed. Today didn't feel like love."

"I made you dinner."

Quest slapped his ass. Hard. "No back talk. I know all your ploys. You think you can make dinner and placate us? It's not happening."

"I can just take my food and y'all can go to hell." This time, Salem literally bit his tongue. He loathed slipping into his southern accent.

"That's better. Be real. You're angry. Tell me why."

"I'm not mad."

Quest slapped his ass again. "Don't lie."

Salem growled. "I'm not mad... at you."

Quest sat him on the island but kept him trapped. He stood between Salem's thighs and held on to his waist. "Now we're getting somewhere. Why are you angry with yourself?" Quest's beautiful, light brown eyes never wavered from Salem.

Salem fought the urge to squirm. He held Quest's stare. He allowed his shell to harden. Salem had to separate himself from this. "You know I'm not a warm person. I'm sorry you expected more."

Quest rolled his eye. "Fucking spare me, Salem. You're one of the most loving people I know. The only time you get like this is when you're scared. We scare you. I know. But the three of us are a family and you don't get to shut down with us. If you need time to deal, then we can live with that, but no more games."

"I'm not playing games." He really wasn't. Salem couldn't handle the destruction they promised. He had rebuilt himself brick by brick. They were too sweet to understand. He cupped Quest's face and kissed him. Salem pulled away and held his stare. "I swear I'm not toying with you. Just please let me deal with things my way. I don't know how to be anyone else."

Like a big kid, Dodge pushed his way in. "Wait. I want kisses too." He froze. "Wait. You two kiss again. I want to watch. That shit was hot as hell."

A laugh burst from Salem. Jesus. These men. They were his soul. No one else made him smile and laugh. Made him happy. He looked Quest's way with raised eyebrows. The hunger waiting for him in Quest's expression took his breath. Quest hauled him closer. Their lips met. A quivering breath escaped him. Quest took advantage and shoved his tongue inside Salem's mouth. He lost himself. Then Dodge pulled his hair, stealing him away. He took over, exploring Salem's mouth. They were both aggressive kissers.

Salem turned his head. "Our food is going to waste."

Quest looked mussed and sexy. "We can eat, or Dodge can fuck you while I fuck him."

Oh, damn. No way would he miss that show. "Definitely the second."

Dodge snatched him from the counter. He didn't bother heading upstairs. Judging by the way Quest prowled after them, they wouldn't make it that far. As they crossed the threshold into his bedroom, Salem told himself he'd distance himself tomorrow. Tonight, he had other plans.

Dodge hadn't been fucked in a long time. He used to love the way Quest always eased him into things and made him beg for more. Tonight, he wanted exactly what Quest's expression promised. He wanted that rough ride. As he gently set Salem on the bed, Quest's body molded against him. His lust shot through the roof. Between the longing in Salem's eyes and the way Quest and Dodge had touched all day, he was more than ready for anything.

Salem worked on divesting Dodge of his clothes. Quest sucked his neck. Dodge was suddenly very thankful for the two morning orgasms that kept him from embarrassing himself. Salem kissed his stomach. Dodge saw stars and rainbows. Happiness choked him. His every sense was overwhelmed.

Quest bit his earlobe. "Salem needs you."

It was like he was a puppet, and everything happened to him. He saw the clothes fly and watched Salem lube his hole. Even as Dodge crawled between Salem's thighs, he felt like everything happened to someone else. Then he was inside Salem. Their tongues fought while Quest played with his asshole. He felt everything all at once, and he was too overwhelmed to move. Quest impaled him with so much force, it rocked him inside Salem. They moaned. All three of them simultaneously made the same sound. It was like a deep need manifested into noise.

Quest moved. They followed. What should have been awkward, and a learning experience, wasn't. It was like they had done this a million times. Maybe they each had in their minds. A love this powerful hadn't started overnight. It was years of starvation and longing. Heated looks. Begging the universe.

Salem scratched his skin and bit him.

Quest kept the rhythm.

Dodge burned. Too much happened to him at once. He was the one in the middle, and he knew he would be the first to blow. Salem felt too good. Quest fucked like a master. Dodge was only along for the ride.

"Goddamn. I can't. Sorry, guys. You're too fucking gorgeous together. I won't—*aghhh*!"

Salem's screamed cry, the way his body sucked him, and the cum hitting him sent Dodge soaring. He couldn't control the sounds he made.

"I'm so fucking in love with you two. You have no idea." Dodge couldn't stop. His mouth rambled while his body jerked. "I've spent so many nights pleading." He finally bit his bottom lip to stop the rambled confessions. The sound of Quest crying out against his shoulder was enough to distract him. They became an exhausted heap of sweaty and cum-slicked bodies. Labored breathing filled the air.

Quest was the first to speak. "Choose a bedroom. We're not sleeping apart again. I love you both too much to handle another night of thinking you'll never really want me."

"I can't move."

Dodge laughed at the genuine exhaustion in Salem's voice. "It looks like Salem has chosen."

A low rumble of sexy laughter vibrated from Quest. "That's fine. Fewer stairs means I can save my cardio for you two."

Dodge felt Salem shake with silent laughter. He couldn't stop smiling.

Dodge honestly hadn't thought this dream would come true. He knew it would take work to keep it. Dodge had never looked more forward to a challenge in his life. Whatever it took. He wouldn't lose these men.

CHAPTER SIX

SALEM TRIED FOR THE third time to tie his bow tie. Dodge kept making a mess of it. A growl rose in Salem's throat. One thing he loved so much about Quest and Dodge was they were giant kids. They made him laugh and allowed his shoulders to relax. Times like now wasn't one of those times.

"Seriously, Dodge. You have to stop. Shaw will be here any second."

Quest curled his lip and looked away.

Dodge bounced on the bed. "Why do you have to go? You should be here with us."

Salem couldn't say, really. He just had to see this through. For one night, he had to show the upper crust he wasn't hiding from them. He just didn't like them. He went with the easier truth.

"I told Shaw I'd go. He knows it's just as friends, and I can't abandon him on such short notice. No one wants to face the sharks alone."

"Do you want us to go?"

At Dodge's question, Quest joined the conversation. "We could get dressed and meet you there. You don't have to do this with just Shaw." The way Quest said Shaw's name left no doubt he didn't like the guy.

"No." Salem felt strongly about this. "I'm doing this with Shaw because it's bad enough I'm doing this. There's no way I'd subject you to those people, and Quest, you know your mom will be there. You don't want to deal with that. I promise I won't stay long. Dinner. A few drinks. I'm out the door."

Dodge pouted for half a second before Salem had to fix it.

"Besides, this gives you two a few hours to move your stuff down here."

Dodge immediately brightened. "That's true."

"We could order pizza, I guess," Quest muttered under his breath, sounding like a moping child.

Salem shook his head. He knew he should find the words to make this right, but he didn't know what to say. Before he could try, the doorbell rang. "Well." He took a breath. "Here I go." Salem headed for the door.

Quest stood and blocked his path. "*Unh uh.* Nope. You're not leaving here without a proper goodbye." Salem went up on his toes and swiped a quick kiss across Quest's lips.

Quest grabbed his waist and took the kiss he wanted, stealing his breath and scattering his thoughts.

"My turn." Dodge practically pounced the moment Quest released him. His kiss was a bit more playful but still had Salem regretting his decision to leave.

Quest moved from blocking the bedroom door. "Okay. Now you can go. We love you. Be good."

Salem smiled at the fatherly speech. "I love you two too. Both of you behave while I'm gone." The innocent smiles he received in return did not set him at ease. Salem truly did not want the two subjecting themselves to society on his behalf. He made his way to the front door, ready to get this over with. Salem was going soft. He should have told Shaw to get fucked. It had only been a week since Quest and Dodge had begun their new lives as his nightly bedmates. He shouldn't risk everything on whatever kept driving him in the opposite direction from them.

He opened the door to a very sexy Shaw. While the guy was always dressed to impress, this was different. He came to slay. Salem couldn't help but smile. He appreciated beauty as much as the next person. "Hey. You clean up nice."

Shaw's smile grew. Laughter flashed in his eyes. "You too. Are you ready to do this?"

With a nod, Salem stepped outside and pulled the door closed behind him before the boys burst outside like overactive guard dogs. They made their way down the front steps.

"Really, though. You look amazing."

At Shaw's compliment, Salem looked his way with a smile. Shaw wasn't quick at hiding his hunger. Salem swallowed a groan. Every time he spent time with Shaw, it felt like a mistake. He was great... for someone else. The guy was a full-ass adult with a good job and his shit together.

He was a gentleman. Someone out there would hit the lottery in him, but Salem had already scored big. He didn't need more.

Still, he needed to keep things light. "You too, seriously. I can tell you pulled out all the stops. Tonight must be important to you for some reason."

They climbed inside Shaw's car. He didn't respond until they were on the road. "Prince Noir is my biggest client. He'll be there tonight with his husband. I have to be at my best. If I ever lose him, my entire clientele will follow."

Honestly, that set Salem more at ease than anything else could have. Shaw wouldn't spend the night trying to get in his pants and Salem was good at rubbing elbows with people like Prince Noir. "You'll do great. I can be charming when I try."

Shaw's laughter let him know he got the joke. Salem hadn't tried with him. Their ride was never silent. They got along well. Salem could see himself with Shaw. Truthfully, that made him a little sad. His heart wasn't up for grabs, but it was poised to shatter. Salem held no illusions. Quest and Dodge wanted each other. Salem was just the excuse they gave themselves to give in to what was already there. Soon enough, they would push Salem out. He would go quietly since he hadn't gone in blindly, but it would hurt. The smart move would be to choose Shaw. Salem would never love him, but love never brought him anything except pain. Calculating each move was better. Control kept him safe.

At the country club where the event was being held, pictures were taken for online gossip sites and as a way to fluff the ego of rich people. That was all any of these events were. Rich people sucking each other's dicks. When they reached the door, Salem fought hard to control his eyes. He wanted to roll them so fucking bad–

ly. They were announcing people's names upon entry like it was an early eighteen hundreds party for the ton. The ridiculousness of the entire event was next level. Still, Salem smiled as people stopped to talk only to—no doubt—run away to speak badly of him. He was relieved as fuck when the dinner portion began. That was until he realized he was seated across from Quest's mother. Luckily, Prince Noir was seated on his left, giving him someone else to focus on, especially since Joesph was also at their table. Shaw kept ordering drinks and grinding his teeth, leaving Salem to be the one who charmed the handsome prince.

Noir had amazing light green eyes that seemed to cut right through people. His husband looked like a biker, which Salem had heard. Seeing him in person was a bit jarring. He looked like a killer. Salem didn't judge. He knew the temptation that drew a man to a hardened body.

The light green eyes swung his way. "Did you know, in my country, poly marriage is legal?"

Salem thought that was an odd–as–fuck random statement, but he was still intrigued. "That's very progressive."

Noir made a dismissive gesture. "It, of course, started as a way for rich men to marry their harems. Then women began to do the same. When my father legalized gay marriage, it made all forms of poly relationships legal as well. We're not the only country in the world with such laws, but it's very uncommon."

"Your father sounds like a good man."

Quest's mom, Ashley, snorted. "Searching for your next husband? We know you have daddy issues."

Salem ran his tongue across his teeth. He had known she wouldn't stay silent all night. "Well, you're the expert on daddy issues. From what I hear, you're on your tenth, so..."

Noir's husband, Lazarus, laughed.

Noir simply looked amused.

Joesph touched her arm. "Would you like another drink?" It was obvious he tried to defuse the situation. It was also the first time Salem had heard him speak all night. When he wasn't enraged, he had a nice voice.

Shaw scoffed. "You're too young for her."

Ashley stood and walked away, looking enraged. Joesph waited half a second before backing his chair from the table and heading in the opposite direction.

"I need another drink." Shaw jumped ship too.

"And then there were three," Salem muttered under his breath and polished off his wine.

Noir laughed. "This has been fun. Usually, these dinners are much more boring."

Salem flashed him a smile. "Shaw said you two would be here tonight. I knew between the three of us we could liven up the place."

The two men roared with laughter.

Heads turned their way.

Something eased in Salem's chest. Despite everything else, he still thought the night had been a success. The prince seemed to like him. He had enjoyed a dig at Ashley. The boys hadn't burst in and made a scene. He remembered there were a few people he liked. Six out of ten stars. He was beyond ready to get home to his comfort zone. Salem eyed the room, searching for Shaw. Considering Shaw's mood, Salem didn't think he would be hard to convince to leave.

"May we, and about a dozen royal guards, walk you to your car? I think this party is about to take a nosedive."

Salem followed Noir's line of gaze. Shaw had Joesph cornered, having a very animated and obviously heated discussion.

"Damn. He drove."

Noir's husband stood. "Even better. We'll drop you at home on our way. We live down the street."

That completely caught Salem's attention. Not only had he not known that, but he also didn't know why Lazarus did. "Really? I didn't realize."

Noir nodded as he stood. "Your late husband used to hold a lot of small gatherings of select people." His eyes flashed with laughter. "They were much better than this one."

Salem was hooked. He fell into step with the pair and headed for the door. "I don't doubt that at all. He was...

the life of the party. I swore he would outlive me."

A guard appeared like smoke and opened the door for them. They were immediately surrounded by more guards. Salem barely noticed. The couple held his full attention. No one ever spoke to him about JD without sneering at him, other than the boys, of course.

Noir flashed him a smile. "He spoke highly of you. JD had an eye for quality, so I was admittedly intrigued to meet you tonight. He said you would ensure his companies continued to run and profit exactly as they always had when he was gone. Truthfully, I thought that was bullshit, but I also know better than to judge a person by their age or where they started. He was right, of course."

In minutes, they were sequestered in the back of a huge SUV. Salem barely noticed. He hadn't expected to enjoy himself this much. Salem's hands rose and fell. "JD was adamant about his wishes. Of course I honored them."

"We should show you where we live. Maybe you can bring your puppies one day and visit."

A smile exploded across Salem's face. No one except JD and Salem referred to Quest and Dodge as puppies. Nothing else could have shown how

well Noir had known Salem's husband. "Are you sure? They can get
pretty destructive."

Lazarus and Noir both laughed.

Salem took a cleansing breath. The
night moved to eight out of ten stars.
He didn't give another thought to
Shaw.

The guy sat on their front porch. He
had been there nearly an hour. Quest
might have gone out of his mind
with worry when Shaw showed up
without Salem. Thankfully, Salem
had immediately answered his texts.

Dodge and he had decided to leave the visibly drunk and enraged visitor outside to wait. They stayed close to the door, though. Just in case. Quest truly hoped Shaw would give up and leave before Salem got home. He didn't want to kick a lawyer's ass. That was likely a lifetime of legal drama he didn't need or want. But when Salem appeared and Shaw shot to his feet, Quest was on his.

Dodge grabbed his arm. "You know damn well it won't end well for you if you go out there. We can afford to win anything he throws at us. But Salem might not forgive you for thinking he couldn't handle himself.

Salem is a badass. He'll take care of this."

Quest settled back down and went back to eavesdropping on the pair through a phone app, showing them everything through the security cameras.

"What the hell? You just left. You didn't even tell me before bailing on me."

Salem looked completely calm. Just as Dodge pointed out, Salem knew how to handle himself. "I did you a favor. You said you couldn't afford to lose Noir as a client. It didn't look like you gave a fuck about that when you were fighting with your man. Thankfully, Noir wanted to reminisce about the parties JD used to throw."

Dodge and Quest exchanged glances. Those had been some wild parties.

"*My man?*" Shaw's outrage had them returning to the drama.

"Yeah. Your man. Surely you don't think I'm an idiot. You don't harbor that much animosity toward someone unless you're fucking, and you were definitely both feet in on Joesph."

"Ha!" The loud, obnoxiously snide laugh made Salem visibly jump.

Quest was back on his feet. Salem needed him.

Dodge pulled him back down.

"You have a lot of goddamn nerve. Don't think I don't know you keep accepting my dates as a way to run from the way you feel about dumb and dumber."

Dodge was the one on his feet this time. They were barely holding each other back.

Except Salem held his own. He went toe to toe with Shaw. His voice came out like ice. "Those two have twice the class you'll ever have. I honestly don't know how you convinced Joesph to have anything to do with you. You're obviously a huge piece of shit and you should definitely find him and kiss the ground he walks on. There's zero chance anyone else sees how ugly you are on the inside and loves you."

"Goddamn." Dodge sat back down.

Shaw stepped even closer, obviously not cowed. "Oh. I see it now. Those poor bastards. Do they even realize you'll never love them? This little ice princess act toward me is just your way of hiding the fact that you're incapable of loving anything except money. I never stood a chance with you because no one does. If I'm ugly inside, what does that make you?"

Salem took a step back. "Realistic. I'm not incapable of love. The opposite, in fact. But no one could love me.

Not really. It's best I don't believe otherwise. If you go to the garage, there's a flight of stairs that leads to the guest loft. Don't drive home and kill someone or ruin your career. I could smell the liquor on you when I hit the sidewalk." He stepped around Shaw and headed for the door.

Shaw threw his hands in the air.

Salem didn't look back.

Dodge and Quest closed the app and immediately headed for the door to meet him. Quest's chest hurt. He supposed he knew Salem felt that way. There was no pretending Salem wasn't a mental mess, just like them. The funny thing was, Salem was the one who couldn't see them. He didn't see how fucked up they were.

When Salem walked through the door, he barely spared them a glance before walking past them and into the bedroom. They exchanged a glance and followed. Salem removed his jacket and bow tie. He untucked his shirt. The entire time he was wooden—like he might snap at any moment. They didn't even look each other's way before wrapping Salem in a tight embrace. A lump grew in Quest's throat at the way Salem trembled.

Salem let the hug go on for a few seconds before pushing his way out from between them. He paced away.

Before Quest knew what would happen, Salem broke.

"FUCCKKK!" He bent at the waist and screamed at the top of his lungs.

Quest and Dodge stood frozen. They had never seen Salem be anything less than controlled.

"Why did I do this?" He tore at the buttons on his shirt, as if he needed to rip something to pieces on his way out of his tux. "I knew better. Three fucking years. I've always known how this would end. You two have each other. You always will. I don't. It's just me and it'll always be just me until the day I die. I was okay. I had accepted that. Then I let this thing tempt me over the edge and now I can hear the goddamn clock ticking."

Dodge looked his way. He looked as devastated as Quest felt. Salem was melting down, and they were useless in the face of it.

"It's only a matter of time before I watch you two realize I'm in the way. I'm just the third wheel in what should be a two-man operation. I fucking knew that, and I still fucked everything up." Salem focused on them and Quest nearly took a step back at the pain he saw in Salem. "I was okay. We were happy." Tears fell from his lashes. "Now I'll be alone again soon. Why did I do that?"

Dodge wrapped his arms around Salem again. Quest quickly jumped in to hold them. This time, Salem stayed lifeless in their hold. It was like he had let go of control for a single minute and it had broken him. Quest didn't know how to fix it. He never knew how to fix anything.

"My mom's death wasn't an accident."

Quest's eyes fell closed at Dodge's quietly spoken confession. "Please don't." Quest couldn't watch Dodge tear himself open too.

Dodge took a breath so ragged and loud, it sounded like it came through a bullhorn. "I have to. He thinks he's alone."

Quest set his forehead on Salem's shoulder and wished to go deaf.

"Women can be predators too."

"You don't have to do this." Salem's voice sounded dead.

"Yes, I do. I knew as soon as you got here. You have that same look in your eyes—like you've seen more than anyone should. My mom wanted nothing more than she wanted a rich man, and I was her ticket. I was pretty, and she kept me that way. She had me distracting wives while she slipped into their husband's beds, doing her best to steal them. JD, well, I don't think he ever really fell for her bullshit, but she was way younger than him and beautiful. Thankfully, he didn't have a wife for me to play with."

"What he had was a son who saw right through her." Quest spoke his greatest shame and chose to take whatever punishment Salem doled. "So, of course, she had to keep me busy."

Dodge took another painful-sounding breath. "Except, this time, it was real. I had never had anyone look at me like Quest—like I was more than a toy."

"I definitely went for all the flirtation, but I wanted more than his body."

Quest couldn't stop adding his side, helping Dodge through exposing the worst of his life.

"So, one night, I told Quest everything. I needed him to know I loved him for real. My biggest fear was him finding out the truth one day and hating me. Mom loved to blackmail me by promising to tell. It was like walking toward my judgment day. I was terrified of losing the only love I had ever known. Like you, it didn't feel like I deserved to have it, so I was doomed to lose."

"But I went straight to JD." Quest still didn't know if he had done the right thing. They could've run away together. There were dozens of choices he could have made, but he had always trusted JD with every big decision. That night had been no different.

"She was dead the next day." Dodge held Quest's stare as he said the words and a weight lifted from Quest's shoulders. He had always wondered if Dodge hated him for telling. Now he knew. He saw the relief in Dodge.

"You know the state took me from abusive parents and placed me with my grandfather. That was true." Salem still sounded dead. "What you don't know is he died a year later, and I couldn't go back to Louisiana. I couldn't go back to..." Salem cleared his throat. He was stiff as a statue in their arms, but he talked, and that felt like progress. "I took all the money I could find in the house and sold everything of his I could. Then I disappeared. His body was still in bed, where he died peacefully, when I walked out the door and didn't look back. I knew if I told anyone, my next stop might be hell. So I just slipped away. It didn't take me long to realize I could charm old men. It started small, a little money for an hour here or there. A lot of money for overnight. No one cared I was barely fourteen. In fact, they liked that. I got bolder, older, and smarter. I found more and more ways to support myself. Then I met Tarek, and he made me want more. He made me want a normal life with a home and friends. He was my age and didn't judge me. When I found out about his awful parents, I helped him escape. Then JD came along, and I swear he saw right through me and liked me anyway. I know no one believes me, but I loved him. It was an odd sort of fucked-up love, but I finally had exactly what I wanted. He had two amazing sons and a beautiful home. I got to cook and play house—like I was a real person and not just the shell I left behind in Louisiana. Then he died and I don't know. You two became my whole life and I don't know how to lose this. I'm not sure I can survive it."

Quest wanted so fucking badly to squeeze the hurt from Salem. He needed Salem to see how real they were, but he didn't know how. Quest just opened his mouth and words fell out. "Do you know why I chose to stay with JD when he divorced my mom?"

A humorless laugh burst from Salem. "I've met her. I understand."

Despite everything, Quest smiled. He heard the hint of life returning to Salem. "It's because I had never been loved before JD. For once, and for real, I had a parent who wanted me. He was already elderly when he married Mom but he acted like a man half his age. He acted like a dad. While Mom was out spending his money, he was taking me to football games and for ice cream. To this day, I'm a thousand percent positive he married my mom and Dodge's because he wanted their sons. He was willing to look like he got used up by gold diggers just to have the sons he never could. But you, I think he married you because you were the one who made him wish and dream. You gave him a normal life—like the spouse he truly wanted for himself. For the last few months of his life, you gave him something he couldn't buy. No matter how much anyone thinks you were bought. We know better."

Quest pulled away and forced Salem to look at him. His nose and eyes were red. He looked like he had been crying all night. Salem looked vulnerable in a way Quest hadn't seen or expected before tonight. "Not one time have I felt guilty for falling in love with you because I knew JD better than anyone. There's nothing he would've wanted more than our happiness." He led Salem to the bed and sat, pulling Salem down with him.

Dodge joined them. "We love you. For real." Dodge sounded desperate to make Salem believe. "This isn't a game of us and you. The three of us are like one soul or something. I can't explain it. We just fit together, and I know you know that. JD found us and brought us together. I won't... I *can't* walk away from us. You two are all that keeps me here. On this planet. Otherwise, I don't know how to live inside this head alone. Trust me, I've had all the therapy and done all the drugs. This is the only place I find peace." He paused. A look of pure devastation touched his features. "But forget I said all that. I won't emotionally blackmail you into loving me the way I need. You can walk away from me if that's what it takes for you to survive. I love you enough to let you go. I love you more than I do me."

Quest couldn't stop switching his gaze between the pair. Dodge was reaching him. Quest watched the steel slowly return to Salem's spine.

"Don't ever say that shit to me again. How dare you think I'd ever feel manipulated by you or leave you?" He looked Quest's way. "Either of you. No matter what, you're the best parts of me, and I won't stop trying to be better."

Quest loved him so fucking much. Salem was the strongest person he knew. He should have known Salem wouldn't stay down for long. The fight returned to eyes a little more by the second. Air finally fully filled his lungs. They were okay. Maybe they were all a little broken, but they sealed each other's cracks and made each other whole. One drunk asshole couldn't break them. Nothing could.

The way Dodge shook inside hadn't happened in years. He was on the edge of a full-blown panic attack, but it was worth it to make Salem see they were all together for a reason. This wasn't some flighty love or fun times. They had a bond no one else could understand. It had just been a long time coming for them to talk about it.

Salem stood and peeled off his shirt. When he went to work on his pants, his eyebrows rose. "Well. Why am

I the only one stripping? I want to snuggle with my babies."

They didn't hesitate to fly to their feet and strip. Dodge needed exactly what Salem offered: a puddle of cuddles. He felt gross and on edge after talking about his mom. Dodge had a ton of mixed feelings. Back when he had been seduced by his very first older woman, Dodge had been old enough to know better and thought it was amazing. He was special. Women couldn't keep their hands off him. He was sexy and irresistible, so age didn't matter. In his heart, he knew his mom hadn't truly thought she did anything wrong with him. After all, men can't be victims. That was bullshit. The older he had gotten, the more he realized how wrong everything felt. He became suicidal and the self-hatred had been deep.

Then he had been thrown in Quest's path. The very thought of being told to seduce a man nearly sent him off a cliff, except Quest was unlike anyone Dodge had ever met. He was kind. It was beyond obvious he had never been chased so hard by another guy. The affection that grew between them felt a hell of a lot like something he had never had. Something pure. Quest didn't take the bait in the way Dodge expected. He loved Dodge for real without the sex and games. It would have been the straw that broke him for Quest to learn why Dodge had thrown himself at Quest. That was why he had been honest. Also, he had just needed help. He had known all the way to his soul that Quest would free him. Dodge didn't know how to say no to his mom. She had too many ways to manipulate him. He had been right. Quest had freed him. But, sometimes, Dodge wondered if it cost Quest his soul. For a few years, Dodge wondered if that was why Quest didn't love him the way he used to. Now Dodge realized it was him who stood between them. He had crawled inside his head and forgotten how to let anyone love him. Dodge had been set on ruining himself because he didn't deserve love. Salem was the same. He lived in his head, guiltily believing he wasn't worthy of this beautiful relationship. The three of them so desperately needed one another. So again, Dodge had bared his soul to save someone. He needed to rescue Salem the way Quest had done for him.

The shaking in his stomach didn't ease until they were nude under the blankets and holding each other. Salem scratched their heads. Dodge listened to him breathe.

"So how did dinner go?" Quest's question had them suddenly laughing, wiping away the dark cloud hanging over them.

"Honestly, it was better than you'd think. I was seated next to Prince Noir and his husband. They salvaged the night by sweeping me away."

"Yeah. JD liked Noir a lot. The feeling always looked mutual. Noir used to be kind of intimidating and scary to be around until he married Lazarus."

"Now Lazarus is the terrifying one," Dodge added, throwing in his two cents.

Salem chuckled. The sound warmed Dodge's chest. A tangle of legs and feet played, making Dodge smile. He couldn't stay quiet.

"I've been in love with both of you for a really long time. I honestly can't imagine a life without you. Can we please stop with the push and pull? I don't know about you two, but I'm exhausted. Life has made me tired. This is the only peace I have." He lifted onto his elbow and held Salem's stare. "When you told us to move our stuff in here, I thought we were finally settled. Now, there's a niggle of fear scratching at the back of my brain again because it's like we're never completely established. It's like I'm just waiting for the other shoe to drop all the time and I hate it."

Salem took a visibly deep breath before slowly blowing it out. "I'm sor–

ry I made you two feel as if you're anything less than my entire world. Even though I really hate when people say it's me, not you, it was me. Not you. I'm determined now, though, and I have a pretty strong spine, so you don't have to worry. One way or another, I will make us work and we'll be happy, because you two are all that holds me together. I won't lose you."

Quest kissed Salem's cheek. "We believe in you."

Love filled Dodge's chest as he stared down at his beautiful men. His eyes stung. He couldn't believe this was real. "I love you both so much." Even he heard the way he struggled not to cry.

Two sets of gorgeous eyes focused on him, looking concerned. "I love you too." The simultaneously spoken words of affection had Dodge struggling even harder. He had to stop before he fell apart. Unfortunately, he gasped for air and realized too late he was already too far gone. Quest and Salem sat up.

Salem eyed him, looking ready to jump in, however needed. "Tell me what to do."

"Take a breath. You're holding your breath."

Dodge did as Quest demanded. His head cleared. Quest was a little more used to Dodge's panic attacks than

Salem. Still, they always made him feel dumb. A lot of things made him feel stupid, but his own body betraying him was a new level.

"Sorry." He took a shaky breath. "You two should kiss or something to distract me."

Quest and Salem exchanged a glance. Salem smirked. They looked his way and all thoughts of coming unglued vanished. He needed whatever they had planned for him.

Salem couldn't explain what happened after his argument with Shaw.

He hated when people shouted. Between Shaw's anger, drunken state, and hateful words, Salem had broken. He had already been under the stress of feeling like he would lose Quest and Dodge any second. Having Shaw confirm his fears—that he was too cold to love—had just been the final straw. There was no way he could have anticipated Dodge and Quest's reaction or confessions. While Salem had known JD married their mothers to have the sons he wanted, he hadn't known how much he had saved them from. Salem should have, though. That was who JD had been. He rescued people who had no chance of saving themselves. Now, Salem felt at peace in a way he couldn't recall feeling. Even when he had gone to live with his grand-father, Salem had lived in constant fear of being sent back to his par-ents. The only time in his life he had felt secure was the three years be-fore his first night with Quest and Dodge. That night had upended him and sent him spiraling. Once again, he had been that kid who knew noth-ing but fear and pain. Salem saw the truth now. That night changed noth-ing. Not really. They weren't hiding any longer, but the love was untouch-able. Unshakable. If anything, they were stronger.

The neediness in Dodge's eyes called to him. So did the helplessness in

Quest's gaze. This was his comfort zone. He could be the glue that held everyone else together.

"Come here." Salem drew them closer. He kissed each one, taking his time and showing his love. "Let's go."

Dodge and Quest looked confused as Salem climbed from the bed. Salem didn't stop. He opened the French doors that led outside to their pool on the beach. Perfect landscaping gave them privacy, but the sound of crashing waves still drowned out all other sounds. He felt the guys' stares upon him as he walked into the pool, nude and ready to play. The boys needed some fun. Being this serious all the time wasn't like them and couldn't be good for their mental health. Two huge bodies cannon-balled into the water, soaking him. They both came up laughing while Salem fought to wipe the water from his eyes. The laughter that filled the air was like a healing balm on his heart. Dodge and Quest didn't stop chasing and dunking him until he cried for mercy. Then he found himself sitting in the hot tub between them with someone's hand on his dick and someone fingering his ass. Salem couldn't say who did what because he was too busy jacking two cocks and fighting two tongues. They moved leisurely. There was no hurry. They had the rest of their lives. Salem couldn't believe how quickly he went from scared to sure of them. This was real. Always had been. They would grow old together, living and loving until they died. The whispered "I love yous" were as endless as they were breathless. When Salem came, he saw their entire beautiful future unfold before his eyes. He sent a prayer of thanks to JD in heaven. Salem knew who he owed for this flawless life. He never forgot it.

CHAPTER SEVEN

THE SMELL OF BACON and coffee had Shaw sitting up in an unfamiliar bed. He blinked at his surroundings until horror washed over him, along with last night's memories. He covered his eyes. Horrified didn't begin to cover how he felt. Embarrassed was in there a lot too. He had really shown out and poured his anger on the wrong person. Still, Salem had saved him from driving home.

He grabbed his phone to check the time. He had missed over half a dozen texts. Shaw opened his messages.

Joesph: *As much as I know I'll regret this, I shouldn't have let you get in your car drunk. Let me know when you get home.*

Joesph: *Please don't make me come check on you.*

Joesph: *It would be great if you'd just put me out of my misery.*

Joesph: *Really starting to worry.*

Joesph: *If this is some way to punish me, I get it, but fuck. This is just cruel. I'd never let you worry like this.*

Joesph: *Damn it. I'm coming to check on you. You'd better stop me before I leave because God help you if I drive all the way across town and you're fine.*

Joesph: *I'm going out my front door.*

Joesph: *You slimy-ass motherfucker. I knew. In my heart, I fucking knew it. As soon as I left, I knew I was making a mistake. I should've just driven by Salem's place first and saved myself from going out of my mind. Lose my number.*

Defeat washed over him. There was no coming back from this one. When it came to Joesph, he was someone else. Someone he didn't like, and he didn't know why. He had to at least apologize, though. Shaw couldn't live with himself otherwise.

Shaw: *I'm so fucking sorry. When I left last night, I was angry and upset. I ended up at Salem's house, needing to scream at someone. He put me up in the guest room and let me sleep it off. I passed out immediately and didn't hear my phone. I'd never intentionally make you worry. No matter what you think, I'm not that big of a bastard. I don't know why I am the way I am, but I get it. I'm destroying your life. If you really want me to lose your number, I will. I just hope like hell that's not what you choose, because that's not what I want.*

Shaw set his phone aside and fought the urge to beat his head against the wall. Every word Salem said to him still rang inside his head. Despite every hate-filled thing Shaw spat at him, Salem still bared his heart and showed vulnerability before saving him from himself. Even while seeing how much his anger obviously scared Salem, Shaw still hadn't stopped. Maybe Shaw was every bit as heartless as everyone always said. He didn't know how to fix it.

Shaw stood. His shoes and shirt were gone. He studied the room. A cursory glance showed him nothing. He pinched the spot between his eyes. Shaw had no clue where he had left over half his clothes. With a growl, he dropped his hand and followed the scent of coffee. Maybe if he begged forgiveness, someone would let him have a cup... and possibly borrow a shirt. How did he end up in situations like this? Sometimes Shaw wondered if he was set on self-destruct.

After following a long hallway, he headed down a set of stairs. When he reached the bottom, the sound of laughter drew him through the sitting room. He found the kitchen. Dodge chased Quest around the kitchen table, snapping a towel at him. Neither of them wore anything more than thin sleep shorts, so his shirtless state didn't feel horribly out of place. The pair didn't notice him right away. Shaw stole the chance to study them. He didn't truly know much about them beyond rumors and what he knew from Salem. While they had all been in Greece together for a week for Tarek's wedding, Shaw had been set on catching Salem's attention, so he had mostly ignored them. There was no denying they were beautiful. They were also full of sunshine. Shaw's throat swelled. This must be a happy home for Salem. It was no wonder Shaw hadn't stood a chance. Plus, goddamn. Those shorts didn't really leave anything to the imagination and whoa. Not only were they beautiful and sweet, but they were also

packing, and damn, some people really got it all.

A warm hand slid across the small
of Shaw's back, startling him. He
glanced over as Salem moved past
him, wearing nothing but a short,
silky robe. Their gazes met. There
was no hatred in Salem's eyes.

"I see you lived through the night. Are
you hungry?"

Shaw cleared his throat, trying to
breathe past the growing lump. He
really had fucked up a lot of shit in
his life. "Yeah. Thanks. I smelled the
coffee."

Salem smiled. "Have a seat, then."

Shaw sat and tried not to look at anyone. He knew the pups hated him. Shaw couldn't blame them.

"How do you take your coffee?" At Quest's question, Shaw forced himself to look at the guy. There was no animosity in his expression. Shaw wondered if either boy was capable of hating anyone. One thing was for sure: Salem was right. They had more class than him.

"Sugar and cream. Thank you."

With a nod, he poured a cup and doctored it before setting it on the table in front of Shaw. Dodge and Salem carried plates of various breakfast foods to the table and arranged them in the center. The three ended up at the coffee station together, filling their coffee cups. Shaw watched them exchange loving looks. Salem leaned Quest's way and kissed his shoulder. Dodge kissed the top of his head. He looked like a man sickeningly in love. Shaw's eyebrows rose when Quest stole a kiss from Dodge. In his heart, he had known the three were together. It was one thing to believe it and another to see it. Not only were they a beautiful throuple, but damn. He would pay good money for that show. Shaw sipped his coffee to hide his reaction. He hated the way his body stirred. The lump was back. He was lonely. Like Salem said, he was ugly on the inside. How could anyone ever

love someone like him? He didn't deserve it.

Quest wasn't the type to kick a man
when he was down. None of them
were. He supposed that came with
being down a majority of their lives.
It was lonely at rock bottom. That
was what Quest saw now that he
looked. Shaw was set on destroying
himself. Likely, even he didn't know
why.

Shaw stood. "I seem to have mis-
placed my shirt. If one of you doesn't
mind loaning me one, I'll get out

of your hair and let you enjoy your meal."

All eyes focused on Shaw.

Quest didn't care enough to argue. He preferred to be alone with his babies.

Salem was always nice, no matter what anyone thought. "Sit down. You should get something in your stomach before you leave."

Dodge obviously felt the same as Quest. "I'm sure I have something you can borrow, but if you prefer, I can help you find your clothes. You were dressed when you got here last night, so your stuff couldn't have gone far."

Shaw dipped his chin. "Thanks. I appreciate the help. I don't relish the idea of wandering through someone else's house. That feels intrusive."

Dodge motioned for Shaw to follow him. "I understand. When I first came to live here, I refused to leave the downstairs unless Quest was with me. I didn't want him to feel like I was intruding."

Quest shook his head as the pair left the room with Dodge chattering away. The moment they were out of sight, Quest snatched Salem from his feet and sat him on the counter. Salem's eyes flashed with laughter as he draped his arms over Quest's shoulders. Quest stood between his thighs and hauled him closer.

"How far do you think I could get before they return?"

Salem's laughter swelled Quest's chest. "Probably pretty far, but we're not about to find out. I'm not giving Shaw a free show."

"We could charge."

Salem laughed harder. His happiness was beautiful.

"At least kiss me."

Salem's laughter died, but his eyes still shone bright with happiness. He held Quest's stare as he closed the distance between them. Quest didn't close his eyes until Salem's lips brushed his. He opened, savoring the moment Salem's tongue swept inside. Quest had given up on happiness. He had given up on this dream until Dodge stirred everything back to life inside him. Now he couldn't stop craving them all hours of the day. He felt the way they grew closer by the minute. Quest was a man in love. His hunger never relented.

Warm lips touched his shoulder. Dodge's hard body molded against him. Quest's every thought scattered. He wanted to beg for these men to swear they would love him forever. Quest wished he could marry them and tie them together forever. He understood that wasn't possible, and it broke his heart a little.

Dodge pulled away first. "Shaw decided not to stay. He's dressing and leaving."

Quest set Salem back on the floor. "I don't blame him. He didn't make any friends last night."

Salem nodded as he carried his cup to the table. "True, but I still feel sorry for him. I don't think he's a bad person, really."

"He's set on burning his life to the ground."

"Exactly," Salem said, proving Quest's thoughts correct.

"He said he was sorry like a dozen times while we looked for his clothes. I know a drunk mouth speaks a sober mind, so I don't doubt for a second he genuinely thinks we're stupid. But I don't think it's personal as much as he just has a huge ego we were stepping all over."

Salem froze with his coffee halfway to his mouth.

Quest swiped a hand over his eyes. He didn't know if Dodge even realized he had just told on them about eavesdropping on Salem's argument with Shaw last night.

Salem set his cup aside. "You were listening." His chest rose and fell on a deep breath. "I suppose I knew you'd heard at least part of what was said since we were yelling. I'm sorry."

Quest honestly didn't understand Salem sometimes. "Why are you apologizing?"

Dodge nodded. "Yeah. Why are you apologizing? You're not the one who called us dumb and dumber."

Salem made a helpless gesture. "You two have—"

"I'm sorry for saying that. You two didn't deserve it."

At Shaw's interruption, all eyes turned toward the door.

Shaw stood with his shoulder leaned against the frame. With his hands shoved in his pockets, he looked like a little kid called to the carpet. Shaw cleared his throat. He sounded and looked uncomfortable as hell. "There's no excuse I can give. All I can say is I have a lot going on right now and you were easy targets at the time." He straightened. "Thanks for everything. I hope you three have an amazing life. You should definitely stop hiding. JD loved a good scandal." With a small smile, he turned away, leaving them alone.

They exchanged glances.

Salem's hands lifted and fell. "I never had any intentions of hiding, so I have no clue what that was all about."

A smile exploded across Quest's face. Dodge looked his way, wearing a matching huge grin. "Well. Let's not let our food get cold over it, then."

Quest grabbed their coffees and moved to sit at the table. They were happy in their bubble and Salem didn't plan to hide them. Things were finally looking up. It was time to eat and get on with the life they deserved.

CHAPTER EIGHT

ONE THING SALEM WOULD always be was a meddler. He couldn't help it. Largely, people were too blind to see what was best for them. When someone was too close to a situation, it clouded their vision. As someone who had been forced to take their power back, he understood how important it was to be brave and reach for more.

As he made his way to the door of a small house, Salem was unsure how he felt. He couldn't see Shaw mingling with anyone poor. Salem was fully aware of what that said about him, but Shaw was... Shaw. Still, Salem couldn't live with any misunderstandings hanging over his head. He had enough genuine wrongdoings to live with. Salem rang the doorbell, fully expecting to be ignored. He wasn't even sure if Joesph was home. Salem shifted from foot to foot and waited. He didn't know how long he should wait. With Joesph in a wheelchair, it could take a minute to get to the door.

When the door swung wide, Salem was more than a little surprised to find himself eye to eye with Joesph. "Oh. I thought you couldn't walk."

God. He heard himself. There was no taking it back. The shock had rendered him stupid.

Joesph's mouth lifted in one corner. He truly was handsome. His light blue eyes swam with humor at Salem's expense. "A lot of people in wheelchairs can walk. It's just exhausting and hard work, but it's even harder work to stay in a wheelchair all day in your home."

Salem could see that. It would be so much more comfortable on the couch with the occasional hobble to the bathroom and kitchen. Salem made a dismissive motion, hoping to move on. "Noir told me where you live. I hope it's okay for me to stop by. It seems my husband used to host these personal gatherings of select people before he passed. At Noir's prodding, I've decided to try to keep his memory alive by continuing his tradition. Maybe not as often, or whatever. Really, this is just a trial. I don't know if I can handle a ton of people in my space." He was rambling. Salem took a breath and pressed on. "Anyhow, it's this Friday. I have an invitation for you. I worried if I had it delivered, you would toss it without even considering attending."

"Why would you even want me there? I'm nobody."

"You were seated with Noir the last time I saw you, and he says he likes you better than most people. Since he was the one pushing me to throw this party, I thought it would be nice if you came."

Joesph shifted his cane from one hand to the next, leaning heavily throughout the entire process. "Do you mind if I sit down?"

Salem felt awful. "Do whatever you need."

Joesph took a step back and swayed.

Without thinking, Salem's arm shot out, giving him something to cling to. "I've got you."

The embarrassment in Joesph's expression tugged at Salem's heart. "Sorry."

Salem tried to play it off. "As some-one who was not born with grace, think nothing of it."

"I call bullshit, but thanks."

Salem followed him inside, closing the door behind him. The living room was small with next to no furniture. It was obvious he had to keep things sparse to ensure a clear path for his wheelchair. Salem intentionally didn't look around. He didn't want to make Joesph any more uncomfort-able than he already was. "Why?"

Joesph looked more than a little re-lieved once he sat. Salem joined him on the loveseat since it was the only choice. Joesph didn't respond until

Salem was seated. "I've seen you several times. You're always flawless in everything you do."

He didn't know what to say or how to feel. "I'm pretty sure I've never seen you before that day at Shaw's office."

A cute smile flashed his way, making Salem want to take care of him. He looked incredibly sweet when he wasn't enraged. "No one looks at people in wheelchairs. We're invisible. I promise we've crossed paths several times."

Again, Salem didn't know what to say. He was kind of angry with himself. Salem liked to think he wasn't like the society he now belonged to. He wasn't one of them. Salem was supposed to be better than what Joesph accused him of being.

"Don't look like that. I don't think it's personal. You get used to no one seeing you."

"Do you?" The question was out there before Salem could stop it. He knew damn well being invisible wasn't something a person grew accustomed to.

Joesph's light gaze swept over Salem's face. "No. That's why I hate these parties. It's just several hours of reminding me of my place."

"You won't go unnoticed. I'll be there. Noir will be there."

Joesph looked away. For a moment, Joesph seemed as if he fought an internal battle. Finally, he met Salem's stare again. "Fuck it. I don't work for Shaw anymore. I don't owe anyone anything. You do realize Noir pushed for this party so he can drum up more business for his drug operation, right? Like, I realize saying that could get me killed, and I have to wonder if that's why Noir asked you to invite me, but yeah. That prince is a king here, running this entire town."

Joesph was right. Someone like him, knowing something like that, could get him killed. Salem didn't think it would happen, though. "Noir didn't ask me to invite you. I'm inviting you because I want you there. As for Noir's drug operation, I'm fully aware of all the players in this town. Not only does my level of income buy everyone's secrets, but JD never would've set me on this chess board unprepared to make a power move, if need be."

"You don't seem bothered."

"I'm unbothered by a lot of things."

"You don't feel used?"

"I'd have to care enough, and I don't," Salem shot back. Exposing himself to someone like Joesph didn't hurt his pride. "I was born in backwoods Louisiana with absolutely nothing and no hope. If I hadn't pulled myself from that place, I would've died there. The people in this town have everything to lose. They have no idea what's it like to starve." Salem never looked away from Joesph. "To trade their body." He needed Joesph to see his spine was steel because he forged it. "I, on the other hand, know all about those things and I've already survived it. They have a hell of a lot farther to fall than I do. So, let them play their games, desperately trying to feel more important than they actually are. It's people like us they should truly fear. We can be one of them, but they could never survive being one of us. If that means they have to peddle their wares, who am I to care? I'll be comfortably chilling with my men while they take turns scrambling for Shaw to keep them out of jail."

Joesph looked away. "Will Shaw be there?"

Salem recognized Joesph had intentionally turned his head to keep Salem from reading his expression. "I'm not sure. He's invited, but I also doubt he's in much of a hurry to see me, since I told him he should apologize to you, and worship the ground you walk on because he was too ugly inside for anyone else to love."

Even without looking directly at him, Salem saw Joesph's mouth lift in one corner.

Joesph looked his way. "Okay. I'll be there. How could I miss seeing the faked shock of seeing you with your *stepsons*?" Joesph threw air quotes around stepsons, but Salem still fought a wince.

"Yeah. I suppose miserable people will always find a way to see the ugliness in love."

"So the three of you really are together?"

"Yes." Salem had to get used to answering that question directly at some point. This seemed like a good place to start.

Joesph's smile grew. "I guess that explains Noir's random as hell comments on poly marriage."

Truthfully, Salem had forgotten all about that. That discussion had gotten lost in the rest of the night. Now that Joesph reminded him, he couldn't think about anything else. "I suppose so." Even to Salem's ears, he sounded distracted. Prince Noir had an uncanny way of knowing everything before anyone else. It was strange and Salem didn't know how to feel.

Dodge had a love–hate relationship with house parties. On one hand, JD had always ensured a night of nothing but fun. On the other, Dodge had a lot of PTSD from the nights he had been paraded past potential targets. He also didn't completely understand why Salem wanted to do this. Not that it was uncommon for him to have no idea what was happening, but still. He knew Salem. Salem didn't party.

From the bed, he watched Quest and Salem get ready. He would wait until the last minute and then wear whatever he wore. Dodge didn't want to impress anyone. "I'm pretty sure I've asked this before, but why are we do-ing this?"

Salem met his gaze in the mirror. He smirked, making Dodge's body stir with a single glance. "Partially, be-cause Noir asked. Mostly, because I want this world to see you two belong to me and I'll crush anyone who tries trespassing."

"Oh. Okay." Dodge fought a happy blush. He remembered now. That was why he had agreed. "You know, every single person you've invited will show up fashionably late."

"Probably not Joesph."

Quest moved to join Dodge on the bed. "Oh. I forgot all about that guy. He's nice."

Salem turned their way. "You know Joesph? I've talked about him before, and you didn't say anything."

Quest shrugged. "I didn't really put two and two together until just now. He's my mom's lawyer."

"Joesph is a lawyer? I guess I assumed he was a paralegal or something."

Quest shook his head. "He handles all the small clients at some big law firm."

"If you mean Shaw's law firm, he quit. I still saw him with your mom at the banquet, though."

"I didn't realize it was Shaw's law firm. But I guess that explains why Shaw always talked like he knew JD. From what I understand, she hired them when JD filed for divorce, expecting such a well-known big-time lawyer would wipe the floor with JD."

Dodge laughed. He couldn't stop himself from joining the conversation. "Of course, JD already had tons of videos of her cheating. He wasn't dumb."

Quest nodded. "Long story short, Mom got tossed down to a smaller attorney in the practice, Joesph, since she stood less than zero chance at winning anything but her maiden name back."

Dodge jumped in again. "After the dust settled, the law firm tried to poach JD as a client from his long-time attorney. He had a lot to say about that."

While wearing an irresistible smile, Salem crossed the room and crawled onto the bed. "I'll bet. JD was fiercely loyal." Salem ran his hand up their chests, looking wicked. "A trait he passed to his boys. One I find super fucking yummy."

God. Dodge had never been happier. He didn't want to have this party, even though he knew it was a way to showcase their relationship. Dodge wanted a quiet night... with some loud moaning.

Salem's hands slid farther down. His eyes flashed with evil intent. Neither Dodge nor Quest could look away. It never took much to have Dodge ready to fuck. That was a good thing, since he had two insatiable men to please.

The doorbell rang as Salem swept over their erections. They both groaned.

Salem popped from the bed, as if completely unbothered by the interruption. "That's probably Joesph. I'll leave you two to cool down."

Dodge planned to make him pay later.

As soon as the door closed behind Salem, Dodge looked Quest's way.

Quest stared at him with the same amount of hunger. Smiles exploded across their faces as they dove at each other. They had to be fast. Guests would flow in behind Joesph soon. Dodge had faith in them. He tore at the front of Quest's pants. In no time, he had Quest's cock in his mouth.

Quest tapped him. "Turn around here. Give me that dick."

Dodge didn't hesitate to flip around so Quest could suck him.

The bedroom door opened. "False alarm. It was just another caterer."

Dodge and Quest pulled away. Guilt raced through Dodge. Salem watched them in silence for a moment, completely expressionless. Finally, he turned away and grabbed a wing-back chair that sat in the corner and dragged it closer. Salem sat. "Don't stop. I like to watch." He unbuckled his belt and slid down his zipper. For a moment, Dodge was hypnotized by the sight of Salem stroking himself. Then Quest sucked his balls, and Dodge forgot his own name. If Salem wanted a show, Dodge had a show for him. He put everything he had into blowing Quest, emboldened by the sensation of Salem's watching eyes on his skin like a physical touch. Dodge made sure Salem saw Quest's cock sawing in and out of his mouth. Saliva ran over his fingers as he stroked while he sucked. The sound of Salem's moans drove him. He wished Salem was in his ass right then. Dodge wanted more. No sooner than the thought hit, Quest fingered him. The sensation at just the perfect moment sent Dodge flying. He fought to focus on his task while he shook with ecstasy. Cum filled his mouth. Dodge automatically swallowed. Salem's cries followed as Dodge still floated on a cloud. Knowing this was forever, that was the biggest rush of all.

People milled from the ballroom to the backyard and back again, going from person to person to chat. Salem looked relaxed. Quest's gaze followed as Salem swept from guest to guest. He felt like he stalked him. His hunger wasn't assuaged. Quest never got enough. Salem and Dodge were a sickness. He never wanted to be cured. Dodge sat with Joesph in the corner, talking animatedly. Once Joesph had shown a genuine interest in their game-making, Dodge was off, talking a mile a minute. No one seemed to even notice them, which Quest found odd. There was never a time when all eyes weren't on Dodge, but it was nice to have a break from worrying about Dodge's safety. Dodge was a muscular guy who could take most anyone in a fight, but he was also the type of person who took spiders outside rather than squish them. His heart was too soft for this world.

Unfortunately, it was like Quest had to fret over something or he wasn't happy. Nearly the moment their fun time ended, guests started showing up, stealing Quest's chance to check on everyone's emotions and soothe his anxiety. He really wanted a drink tonight. It didn't help that the scent of liquor permeated the air, and Quest was scared shitless about Salem's feelings.

Salem had spent a lot of time hiding his fear of being the third wheel. They tended to stick to making love when all three were present. At least, that had been the norm since Salem's breakdown. While Salem hadn't seemed upset earlier, and had joined in his own way, there was a nervous flutter in Quest's gut. He couldn't lose Salem. He tried to be the one who stayed in tune with everyone's emotions, so he didn't fail anyone. Not getting to talk to Salem was killing him.

The first moment Quest saw Salem alone, he snagged Salem's waist and hauled him into the nearest empty room.

Salem laughed and then moaned as Quest claimed his mouth.

Quest forgot why he had started this until Salem gently untangled himself.

"What's wrong, baby?"

He searched Salem's features, looking for any signs of hurt. Quest hated the thought of making Salem feel pushed out. Until that moment, he hadn't realized exactly how big of a wreck he had become over the last few hours. "Please don't be mad at me."

A line appeared between Salem's eyebrows. "Seriously, sweetie. Tell me what's up."

"Earlier. I didn't mean to make you feel like a third wheel or anything. I don't know how—"

Salem kissed him, cutting off his speech. "Stop, angel. Like I said, I adore watching you two together, but even if I hadn't come back, we're good. I know there'll be times when it's you two, or us, or Dodge and me. That's what we signed up for when we chose this road. It fills my heart to know you two have each other. Are you up–set when I'm alone with Dodge?"

Quest's nose immediately curled. The question irritated the hell out of him. "No. Why would I be?" He paused, an image of Dodge and Salem get–ting the same action Quest had ear–lier flashed through Quest's mind. Damn. He wanted that. "Fuck. Why did we invite all these people? I want to watch you with Dodge."

Salem laughed. Happiness flashed in his gaze. "See? We're good. Perfect, in fact. Come on. I need to talk to you both about something."

Salem dragged him from the room while Quest still stared into space, seeing Salem's pouty lips wrapped around Dodge's cock in his mind. For real, he needed all these people to go home. He spotted Dodge wondering aimlessly and looking like a lost puppy. Dodge's entire body lit when he spotted them. He skipped to their side.

"Hey. I couldn't find you."

Salem's smile matched the way Quest felt. It was impossible not to smile when Dodge was like this. He lit the entire room with his unbreakable spirit. Dodge was sunshine and hope in a bottle.

Salem took Dodge's hand while still holding Quest's in his other. He looked between them. "I was just telling Quest I needed to talk to you two. There was a bit of an ulterior motive on my part for this party."

Prince Noir moved close with his husband at his side. Quest cast them a quick smile, but he refused to interrupt Salem, even for royalty.

Salem motioned Noir's way. "The night Noir and I met, he told me a fascinating story about the laws in his country. It seems poly marriage is legal there, but you either have to be a citizen or have your marriage blessed by at least two royals." He waved toward Noir and Lazarus again. "Well, we have two royals, Prince and Prince Consort Antonsen.

So." Salem dropped to one knee. A couple of audible gasps rumbled from their onlookers. Salem produced two ring boxes. "Will you marry me?"

Holy shit. As crazy as it seemed, at no point did Quest know where that speech was headed. He had pushed marriage from his mind since he hadn't thought there was any chance of that life. Quest sure as hell wouldn't marry either man without the other.

Quest looked Dodge's way.

Dodge appeared every bit as floored. "Are you serious?" He looked Noir's way. "We have your blessing?" His gaze swung Quest's way. "Am I being punked right now?"

Quest couldn't stop smiling. "I'm pretty sure he's serious and I'm definitely in."

"Me too. Holy shit."

Salem laughed, making Quest realize they had left him on one knee while they flipped out. At the same time, Dodge and Quest pulled Salem to his feet. They didn't let Salem take a breath while they bombarded him with kisses. Quest felt too much. He couldn't stop touching his men. They may as well have been alone for all Quest noticed anyone outside their bubble.

Noir waited to interrupt until after they had put on their rings and stolen more kisses. Dodge kept swiping tears away, breaking Quest's heart. He understood. They would be a family for real. It meant so much more than anyone could ever imagine.

"You'll have to come to Serveno to wed and the U.S. won't recognize the legality of your marriage, but your marriage will still be very real. It is nothing to change last names."

Dodge looked Quest's way. They held each other's stare. It didn't need to be said. They already knew. In their hearts, they had always been Rochesters. Now they had the excuse they needed to be that for real. There were no words.

As if they planned it, all three stepped closer at the same time. They put their heads together. With their eyes closed, they simply shared a bubble no one could penetrate.

"I love you."

Salem's whispered words brought tears to his eyes.

"So fucking much," Dodge added.

Quest took a shaky-sounding breath. He squeezed his men tighter. "For the rest of my life."

It had always been them. Now they would officially be forever. Quest couldn't ask for more.

CHAPTER NINE

THE NIGHT BECAME A blur of champagne and congratulations. When it finally wound down, and it was only a select few friends left, Salem's shoulders relaxed. Six chairs surrounded the small table inside the kitchen, Salem at one end and Lazarus at the other. Dodge and Quest sat on the right and left of him. Joesph and Noir sat on the right and left of Lazarus. In the center of the table, along with a few open liquor bottles and filled glasses, sat the infamous Two Dares game. Salem eyed the deck, wondering how and why they were doing this. It seemed Noir had made a valiant effort to get to know the boys. From there, it hadn't taken long for them to confess their secret career. Then, somehow, here they were. Salem had no idea how this would go or where it would end. All he knew was it wouldn't be the same as last time.

This time, it turned out Joesph was the oldest. Somehow, miraculously, they had already made one loop around the table without anything lewd happening.

Joesph drew his second card and read, "Hop on one foot or text your crush." Joesph looked down at the wheelchair he sat in and chewed his bottom lip.

Dodge jumped in to save him. "That one is a bit unfair. You can draw another card."

Joesph shook his head. "It doesn't say what I have to text them." He picked up his phone and typed for a moment before setting his phone facedown again. "There."

Thankfully, no one was nosey enough to ask who or what Joesph had texted.

Dodge drew the next card. "Tell your biggest secret or tell the person to your right how you really feel about them." Without missing a beat, Dodge looked Joesph's way. "It was really great talking to you tonight. I hope you want to be friends."

Salem's heart squeezed. Dodge was such a beautiful soul. It was hard to make friends as an adult and it definitely wasn't easy to ask someone to be your friend without sounding like a five-year-old. Salem loved him.

Joesph smiled. It was genuine and lit his eyes. "Absolutely."

Salem grabbed a card before anyone dared make Dodge uncomfortable. "Do the entire Electric Slide or take five shots of the nearest liquor." There was less than zero chance Salem would do the Electric Slide. Luckily, there were already a few bottles of alcohol on the table he could stomach straight. Salem grabbed one and Dodge jumped up to get him a shot glass. He poured the first shot of tequila and quickly did all five while everyone counted loudly.

Lazarus blew out a low whistle. "Damn. You didn't even flinch."

Salem laughed, hoping to hide the way his head already spun. "This is the good shit. I worked in casinos my whole adult life before marrying JD. I've drunk a lot of shots."

Quest shook his head. "Maybe stop there just the same. You don't weigh enough for all that."

Salem snorted but didn't argue. He wasn't a big drinker any longer.

Quest drew the next card. "Do a backflip or tell an uncomfortable story about yourself. Well, fuck. I'm too old to be doing backflips."

"Not to mention you can't do a backflip."

Everyone laughed at Dodge's interjection.

A big, goofy smile lit Quest's face. "True." He tapped the card on the table and stared into space, as if trying to think of a story. Finally, another smile passed over his lips. "When I was six, my mom introduced me to JD. It's important to note I don't know my dad. If my mom knows who he is, she never told me, and we don't talk anymore because I chose JD over her." Quest used air quotes around the last part. Salem got it. She was fucking childish. "Anyhow, I didn't know my dad, so obviously, I didn't know his family. So when Mom was all, 'there's someone I want you to meet.' All I saw was an old man. A man old enough to be my grandfather. Hell, maybe my great-grandfather. So, of course, I got all excited and yelled, 'Are you my grandad?'" A loud bark of laughter burst from Quest. "My mom beat me for that."

Salem's smile fell at that last tidbit.

Joesph's phone loudly buzzed on the table, saving Salem from saying all the words clogging his throat and ruining the night. Joesph turned over his phone and read his text. His face stayed completely blank. "Well, guys. I hate to bail on you, but it looks like I need to head home."

Dodge stood. "Do you need a ride? I don't remember if you've had anything to drink."

Joesph's expression turned sweet. "Thank you, but no. Stay. Enjoy your game."

Dodge nodded.

Noir stood. "I hate to abandon you too, but it's late."

Everyone came to their feet.

Salem followed them to the door, saying his final goodbyes. A wave of relief washed over him when he shut the door behind them. He was beyond ready to have his peace back. The kitchen was empty when he returned. Their cleaning staff would pick up the mess, so Salem left it behind and went in search of his men. The light was on in the bedroom, so Salem started there. The room was empty, but the French doors stood open. Through the doorway, he saw Dodge shirtless and staring at the sky. Quest was nowhere to be found. Salem made his way outside. He didn't want to disturb Dodge, but he equally needed to touch him. Salem molded against his back. With his cheek pressed against his skin, Salem ran his hand up Dodge's chest until he covered Dodge's heart. He savored the steady beat.

"Sometimes, I just stand out here and think about how small I am."

Salem's eyes stung at the wonder in Dodge's voice. He was so much more than anyone saw. His mind was beautiful.

"There's so much out there. I wonder if anyone else thinks about that—like how we're not even a speck by comparison. Yet I still believe you're part of me. I still think this isn't the first lifetime where I loved you and Quest. It's like I knew you two already when we met, and I know I'll find you both in the next life. I just don't understand how less than a speck ended up blessed like that."

Salem could barely swallow past the lump in his throat. Then Quest's arms wrapped around them and Salem's eyes closed. He realized he wasn't scared. Salem didn't need to guard himself in any way. Because Dodge was right. They had loved each other before, and they would love each other again. Maybe that sounded crazy to some people, but not him.

"I just came out here to let you know I'm about to take a shower." Quest kissed his shoulder.

"Okay, sweetie."

He felt Quest smile against his skin before he pulled away, leaving Salem and Dodge to their stargazing.

Salem kissed Dodge's spine.

Dodge's hand covered his. "You should join Quest. I want to spend a few more minutes thanking the universe."

Love filled Salem until it nearly drowned him. Still, he took a step back. "I love you."

Dodge flashed a sweet smile over his shoulder. "I love you too."

Salem headed for the door.

"Hey."

Salem turned at Dodge's call.

He found Dodge staring at him with that same flood of love. "Thank you."

Salem smiled. "I thought you were thanking the universe tonight."

"I am."

Salem's throat swelled. "You never have to thank me."

"Yes, I do." Dodge went back to staring at the sky.

Salem forced himself to leave Dodge behind. He understood the need to have a moment from whatever powerful thing it was the three of them shared. They had an overwhelming love. Sometimes it was almost too heavy.

He slipped into the bathroom. Inside the wet room, Quest sat on the bench and let the shower heads blast him from every direction. He, too, seemed to stare at nothing, completely lost in thought. Salem didn't undress. If Quest wanted peace too, then Salem would make himself scarce.

He peeked open the door. "You good?"

A sweet smile turned his way. "Yeah. I was just waiting for you."

"Are you sure? You look like a man who wants to be left alone."

Quest rolled his eyes.

Salem couldn't stop smiling as he stripped.

"I was a bit lost in thought, though."

Salem paused with one foot in the wet room.

"You should have an engagement ring too. It should match, but I wasn't sure if I should just ask where you got ours or try to drop hints. Then I decided you're the straightforward one, so I should just ask."

Salem shook his head. He was so in love with this man. As he had once said to Dodge, Quest was the 'everyone gets love in this house' guy. It never got old.

Salem closed the distance between them. "They were specially made by Grant Cullier."

Quest blew out a low whistle. "Damn. Really? I thought it took months to get him."

Since Grant was the most famous jeweler in the country, that was true. "Not when you have money like ours. I got all three rings, so they'd match."

Quest tugged Salem down into his lap. "I expect you to wear that ring."

Salem held up his hand, showing he already wore his. "I put it on earlier. When you went upstairs to get the game, I dipped in here and grabbed it." They put their hands together, studying the rings side by side. Quest settled deep into the corner, with Salem held against his chest. Salem listened to his heartbeat as he stared at the matching rings. His throat swelled.

"I genuinely can't wait to be married to you two. It's been hard as hell, pretending I didn't want this while you two chose everyone else but me."

A sharp laugh burst from Quest, confusing Salem. He looked up. Quest shook his head. "Dodge and I had the same fucking conversation about this. Almost word for word. It's like we're all stupid or something."

They weren't. "No. Just scared. I'm not anymore. I know we're unbreakable."

The shower door opened. A nude Dodge stood on the other side. "Can I join the cuddle puddle?"

He sounded so adorable.

Quest lifted his arm.

Salem lifted his legs.

Dodge slid into place. The three of them clicked together like Legos. They sat in silence, enjoying the hot water and each other. Their fingers played as they quietly mused over the rings on their hands. He didn't know how long it would take for Noir to set things in motion for their marriage, but it couldn't come fast enough for him. He was in love. This was forever.

Keep an eye out for the next Atlantic City's Most Wanted, *Single Greatest Threat.*

ABOUT THE AUTHOR

CHARITY PARKERSON IS AN award-winning and multi-published author with several companies. Born with no filter from her brain to her mouth, she decided to take this odd quirk and insert it in her characters. One of her greatest loves is writing morally gray characters. You'll find them scattered throughout her hundreds of titles.

*Nine-time Readers' Favorite Award Winner

*2015 Passionate Plume Award Finalist

*2013 Reviewers' Choice Award Winner

*2012 ARRA Finalist for Favorite Paranormal Romance

*Five-time winner of The Mistress of the Darkpath

Connect with her online:

*Sign up for her newsletter: https://bit.ly/charityparkersonnewsletter

*Join her readers' group on Facebook: http://bit.ly/CharitysTribe

*Website: https://www.charityparkerson.com

*A list of her social media accounts and giveaways all in one place: http://hy.page/charityparkerson